THE EXILE

THE EXILE

The Dry Earth Series Book 2

by

Donald Levin

Poison Toe Press

2020

Inquiries should be addressed to
Poison Toe Press
PO Box 206
1221 Bowers
Birmingham, Michigan 48012

ISBN-13: 978-0-9972941-6-3

First edition published 2020
Printed in the United States of America

For Andrew Charles Lark and Wendy Sura Thomson, without whom this book would never have been written.

Author's Note

The present work is a self-contained, stand-alone companion to Book 1 in the Dry Earth Series, *The Bright and Darkened Lands of the Earth*. *The Exile* describes eight days in the life of Mae, one of the characters from Book 1, following her exile from the underground settlement where she lives with her tribe in a bleak post-apocalyptic future.

It is not necessary to have read the first book to enjoy this second one. But if you liked this book, I invite you to read Book 1, which you will find in an anthology of three dystopian novellas: *Postcards from the Future: A Triptych on Humanity's End* (Whistlebox Press and Quitt and Quinn Publishers, 2019). Also included in that volume are excellent, gripping, and thought-provoking works of dystopian fiction by Andrew Charles Lark and Wendy Sura Thomson.

Postcards from the Future: A Triptych on Humanity's End is available in paperback and Kindle versions through www.amazon.com and on order where ever books are sold.

1

And she's awake.

A muffled noise, a whisper of rag-wrapped feet on the dirt floor, some words of murmured instruction: these pull her from sleep. In a sweat, heart pounding. The sounds are not loud, but she has always been a light sleeper; even with only one good ear, she could be awakened by the echoes of distant noises in their underground settlement back when she was a child, imagining monsters.

Now Mae is an old woman and she doesn't have to imagine the monsters. They are real, and already here. Wandering in the Upground.

And sometimes down below, in her underground settlement, too.

Sitting up, she is surprised that she has even fallen asleep. After the meeting of the Council of Elders, of which she is part, she had lain awake for most of the night, worrying over whether to tell Odile about what had happened.

Odile is the chief elder of the Council, as well as her companion. The other members of the Council did not let Odile know about the meeting, and made Mae swear she would say nothing to Odile until the Council as a body could speak with her.

It was a brutal, unfair request to make of Mae, and what the Council decided was equally unfair. After agonizing about it for most of the night, Mae had decided she needed to let her companion know about it, regardless what she had promised.

Mae looks over at Odile's mat. Her friend is still asleep, a small bundle with a grey head protruding from her tattered cover. It is cool and airless in their underground settlement, but Odile is old—older than Mae—and gets chilled easily.

Mae watches the rise and fall from her companion's breathing. The sound that woke her did not come from Odile.

Mae looks around the room where they sleep. In the dim light from the lantern out in the tunnel, all seems quiet.

She lies back, adjusts her aching bones on her sleeping mat, and closes her eyes.

She tries to calm herself. Whatever dream she had been having (now dissipated entirely) and the tense Council meeting of the night before have left her with a deep feeling of unease.

She opens her eyes and stares at the support beams crisscrossing the rock overhead.

Now fully awake, she begins to feel the familiar pressure in her bladder, and decides she must find her way to the sanitation chamber to relieve herself before she can try to get back to sleep.

She makes her way down the tunnel outside her room to the foul-smelling chamber, where she squats over the trench in the dark. She rinses her hands in the water standing in a bowl carved into the rock walls, and goes back out into the tunnel. It is lit, as all the corridors are at night, by the flickering light of a small lantern.

That's where they take her.

Someone comes up from behind and pins her arms in a bear hug. She struggles, but she is held fast.

Someone else—she can't say who because they approach her from behind—ties a rag over her mouth and throws a hood over her head. The material of the hood is threadbare, like most of what they own in the settlement, and it lets in some of tunnel dim light but not enough for her to make out who her attackers are.

One of them strikes her over the head with a heavy object, not hard enough to knock her out but with enough force to make her old legs wobble and let go from under her. The arms that pin her release her and she is allowed to fall to the ground, heavily and clumsily.

2

The fight goes out of her, along with her breath.

Dazed and winded, she feels hands grasping her roughly and half-carrying, half-dragging her down the tunnel away from the sanitation chamber and her own sleep chamber. She is too confused to figure out which direction they take her.

At last, she feels her attackers pushing her up an incline. She panics. It must be the passageway to the Upground.

Why are they taking her there?

She tries to shout, but with the rag across her mouth she can only emit a high screech. She tries to shake herself free but the hands that hold her are too strong.

Can anyone hear her?

Can anyone *help* her?

Her shins bang and scrape against the rocks on the ground as they pull her up the passageway. She is still barefoot and wearing only the nightshirt she sleeps in.

She can feel the air warming as they drag her up from the underground and rise to what was once the entrance of the nickel mine where they have made their settlement.

Finally, they bring her to the opening. She can feel the full heat of the above-ground world through her thin clothes and the flimsy hood on her head.

She hears her attackers exchanging words with the entrance guards. Their voices are low and urgent, but she can't make out what they are saying.

She is pulled over the rubble that surrounds the entrance. The jagged old concrete blocks, bricks, bent and burnt wood slats join with the remnants of old weeds and branches from the dead trees to cut and scrape her bare feet and legs as they pull her away from the settlement.

Disoriented, she has no idea how far they drag her. At one point, her attackers pick her up off the ground—she is old and malnourished and does not weigh much—and she feels them begin to trot with her.

They go on like that for what feels like hours.

When they finally stop, they let her fall to the ground and pull the hood from her head. It is still night, but the sun never sets in the far north where they live, so the sky is a dim golden color. The sun of early morning makes her squint so she still can't tell who has taken her, but she hears them panting from the exertion of carrying her.

She lies on her back. Someone unties the rag from around her face. Her mouth is dry, cottony, bitter with the oily taste of the cloth. She tries to scream, protest, call for help, but her tongue doesn't work and all that comes out is a hoarse croak.

A face looms close to her own. She sees it is Cyn, one of the security squad. Cyn cradles her head and holds a container of water to her mouth. Thankful, Mae drinks. It loosens her tongue enough for her to rasp, "Cyn, why do you do this?"

"Sorry, elder," Cyn replies. She lets Mae's head down and sets the water container on the ground beside her.

"Come," another woman barks. "Leave her!"

Cyn gets up but Mae grabs at her cloak. "Wait!"

Cyn gently pries Mae's hands free. The other woman now looms over Mae. Mae recognizes her as Meela, the leader of the security work group. In the light of early morning, Meela's eyes are black, the color of pitch darkness underground.

Glowering down at Mae, Meela says, "Know this, elder Mae. You suffer banishment from the settlement by order of the Council of Elders."

"No," Mae protests, her voice still rough from the rag that was wound around her mouth. "That would never happen. Odile is the chief elder. She would never—"

Meela holds a hand up to cut Mae off. "Nay appeal," she says, "nay protest. If you return, you will be dragged up."

Killed.

"How can this be?" Mae asks. She is an elder herself, as well as Odile's companion—when did the Council take this vote? She was present at the last secret meeting, and this never came up. How would Odile ever agree with it?

Mae tries to sit up, but Meela puts a foot on Mae's shoulder and kicks her down flat onto the red dust of the ground.

"Come," Meela orders Cyn.

"Cyn," Mae cries, "nay go!"

The two women ignore Mae's pleading. They jog away without looking back.

2

Mae rises unsteadily and tries to follow them, but the cuts and scrapes on her soles and legs are too painful and she can't go very far before she stumbles and falls.

Soon her abductors are out of sight amid the dirt and dead trees of the dry landscape.

Mae looks around. She does not recognize anything. Years before, she was a Venger and roved the Upground often. Now she can't remember any of it. She thinks she might be several klicks away from the settlement entrance, but she can't be sure how far they carried her.

She wants to scream, sob, cry out to Odile to come rescue her. But she knows Odile will not. Odile will be too busy trying to deal with what the Council has done to *her* to worry about Mae.

Besides, the Council will not permit it. Mae knows she has been given the ultimate penalty that the tribe can enforce: banishment with no protection against the harsh sun and radiation, and no food or water to help her survive. It is meant to be a death sentence without the violence of actually killing her.

Odile will not come and save her, she knows. Once she realizes what has happened to them both, Odile will want to come after her, but the Council will not allow it, and Odile may even be detained to prevent her. Banishment is permanent.

Now she sits on the rocky ground until she regains control over herself. She must think clearly about what has just happened and what she can do.

How she can go on.

How she can survive.

Mae notices that Cyn has left the container of water with her. She hopes Meela did not see that, because helping the banished one is itself punishable by banishment.

It is early morning, but the day is already starting to heat up. She must find some shade. In the dead land, there is no live vegetation of any kind left. Some dead trees still stand, skeletal silhouettes of trunks and branches, barren of leaves. They are Mae's only chance for a bit of shade from the unforgiving sun.

Before she can find shade, however, there is one thing she must do first.

She was taken without any clothes except the nightshirt she wears. She needs to do something about coverings for her feet.

She tears two strips off the bottom hem of the nightshirt and ties them around her bleeding feet. There are no longer any ointments for the cuts she sustained when Cyn and Meela dragged her off, and she has seen enough people come into the settlement from the Upground in a similar shape to know that it is only a matter of time before her wounds come infected.

She tries to push that notion from her mind and takes a long drink.

Still, she cannot help herself. Her thoughts fill back up with how dire her situation is . . . no food, little water, no protection from sun or heat or radiation . . . the probability of infection is the least of her worries.

With her feet bound as well as she can get them, she tries to stand.

The ground feels as if it is tilting. Her balance is off—did she get a blow to the head during this ordeal? She can't remember—but she stands well enough to teeter across the dusty landscape toward a copse of dead trees. They will provide her with enough shade to keep her brain from frying as the early morning turns to morning and then day, when the full strength of the sun in the thin atmosphere begins to beat down.

When she reaches the trees, she throws herself against the flaking trunks, and slides down. Her feet are terribly painful; she stretches them out in front of her and tries to position herself where the shade is fullest. It is not adequate—her bare arms stick out from the narrow strip of shade cast by the bare trees—but it is better than nothing.

Think, Mae, she orders herself.

What are her choices?

She could stay, and wait to drag up from thirst, starvation, or exposure.

She could try to return to the settlement.

Meela made it clear to her she would be killed if she returned. She knows that is the truth; the guards at the entrance will kill anyone who has either been banished or who seems like a threat, no matter who. Mae would not be the first person killed by the guards.

Even if she is an elder.

Or *was* an elder. Banished, she is no longer a member of the community, let alone the elders' Council.

Of course, she thought bitterly, if she hadn't been an elder, she wouldn't be in this situation in the first place.

She is only here now because she refused to take part in the Council's overthrow of Odile as chief elder in the secret meeting of the night before. Another of the elders, Ells, took over as chief elder. She must have been the one who ordered Mae's banishment as another way of striking at Odile's support in the tribe.

Well, Mae thinks, if I can't go back to the settlement, I will not stay here and wait to die. I will find someplace to go.

She tries to remember what the area looks like.

Odile has a map of the land, but Mae cannot visualize the details of it this far from the settlement no matter how hard she tries. She has not been in the Upground for years; when she grew too old to serve as a Venger, she took on other tasks and had no reason to go Upground anymore.

Members of the Council of Elders rarely venture Upground. They are too old to manage the dangers. They send their younger members to perform the tasks outside their underground home.

Primarily, that meant the Vengers, who would scavenge the ruins of civilization for the increasingly sparse stores of food or items that could be useful, and the Vesters, who go out to harvest any food the Vengers might find. Most of the other members perform tasks related to the safety and welfare of the tribe within the depths of the former nickel mine that now serves as their home.

In her youth, Mae was trained as a Venger. She does not know exactly how old she is—time is no longer calculated as it had been in the Before—but she thinks she might be in her fifties. But they live a rough life, and she feels *old*.

She spends the rest of the day among the dead trees, moving around them to follow the shade as the sun tortures the landscape.

At one point, her exhaustion overwhelms her and she sleeps.

When she wakes, half of her body is in the full light because the sun had continued moving while she remained immobile. She already feels the sting of the burn on her upper arm and forearm.

She scrambles back into what little shade she can find.

She leans her head against the scratchy trunk of the tree and closes her eyes. She tries to think her way through to some solution for her situation.

She's not sure there is one.

When she opens her eyes, she discovers one more problem.

A raggedman is crouching in a gully a few meters away.

Looking right at her.

3

Like all of his kind, he is dressed from head to toe in whatever clothes he has been able to scrounge from the living or the dead when he encountered them. His head is wrapped so that only his eyes are visible. Every other piece of skin is covered. In the long run, she knows the rags alone won't protect him from the radiation that poisons the air in the aftermath of the Large War, one of the catastrophes that desolated their world. But it will offer some protection against the harmful rays of the sun. The thin atmosphere allows most of the dangerous rays through to damage whoever spends time outside.

Some raggedmen wear dark glasses, but he has none. His eyes are hidden in the depths of the rags.

As she watches, he stands and begins to make his way toward her. The rest of his body, from his shoulders to his feet, is also wrapped in layers of rags. Despite the heat, wandering in the Upground requires people to protect as much of themselves as they can.

That is why Mae is in such danger. She wears only her thin sleep garment. Never mind that she had no food and the water will soon be gone. She will drag up from exposure before starvation or dehydration finish her.

The raggedman carries a staff, which he leans heavily on as he approaches. He limps, she notices, favoring his stiff right leg.

She knows she does not have the energy to flee from him. And she has nothing to use to protect herself. She is as defenseless as an infant.

As Cyn and Meela intended.

As the Council of Elders meant her to be in her exile.

Let this raggedman come, she tells herself. She will put up what useless fight she can, but in the end this will be over quickly.

As he approaches, she can smell him. Raggedmen have a particular smell, a sour odor of stale man-sweat on bodies that never wash, plus a burned-metal scent that could be from radiation that seeped through pores into bones and dyed them the dark brown color she has seen so often before in the bodies of raggedmen who made their way—or were brought—to the settlement.

She remains where she is, seated against the bare trunk of a dead pine tree. At this northern point, near what used to be Thompson, Manitoba, most of the bark has either fallen off or been burned off and all that are left are the smooth trunks of the trees.

She steels herself to resist, if only for a few seconds before the end.

The raggedman pauses several meters away and looks down at her. He seems to take in her lack of clothing, the flaccidity of her muscles, the look of exhaustion and despair on her face.

Do your worst, she thinks.

He approaches and pauses beside her. He lays down his staff and removes his outer cloak. It is caked with dust and filth. Underneath it he is wearing another cloak. She wonders how many layers he has on.

He snaps it a few times to remove the surface grit, and, gently, steps forward and bends down to wrap it around her.

Then he backs a step away. "You need," he says, using the terse form of language that has evolved for communication, especially between strangers.

"Why give?" she asks.

"You need," he repeats.

She stares into his eyes, visible at this close range between the rags over his face and the rags on his head. His eyes are black and depthless.

He sits down heavily beside her. He stretches his right leg out in front of him and she can see that the leg is false from the knee down, a length of wood carved from what remains of the trees. The end near his knee has been grooved to receive his stump, and the other end is bent to receive a tattered shoe.

He takes several rattling deep breaths and turns his head to look at her. He raises both hands in a gesture of peace.

"No hurt," he says. He pats the air. "Safe."

"Thank you," she says, "for the cloak. But who are you? Why do you do this?"

He stares at her as though revising his opinion of her because she has used the old-fashioned syntax.

When he doesn't answer, she says, "I am Mae."

He nods, repeats her name.

"And you?" she asks.

He shakes his head, as though the answer doesn't matter.

When she sees he is not going to reply, she asks, "Where are you from?"

He looks off into the distance. "Not far," he says. "You?"

"Also not far," Mae answers. She cannot point in the direction of her settlement because she does not know where it is.

Then he says, "I am looking for a girl. Young. Small, seven years. Have you seen her?"

The expansion of his own language takes her by surprise, as does his request. She stares at him, trying to divine his intent. A man wanting help to find a girl is not a good thing. Men want little girls for only a small number of reasons.

She asks, "Why?"

Now he gazes at her, as if trying to decide how much to tell her. Finally, he looks away and says, "She is my daughter."

Does Mae believe him? It doesn't matter, because she hasn't seen any girls—or anyone at all—in the Upground all day. There aren't any inside her settlement, either.

She shakes her head. "I have seen no girls today."

He accepts that. After a few moments, he raises a finger to the sun. "Dangerous out here," he says. "Danger, aye?"

"Aye. I know danger."

He nods, satisfied, then slowly gets to his feet. He holds onto the tree and loosens up his good leg.

"Goodbye," he says. He begins to walk away, slowly, limping on his artificial leg.

Though she feels a surge of relief at his leaving—she still does not entirely trust this raggedman who is looking for a girl—she is simultaneously panicked that someone who may be her only chance for help is going.

She says, "Wait!"

Without turning back, he waves an arm and continues on this way.

She sits for a moment longer, watching him disappear over a rise. Soon he is gone, and she wonders if she has imagined this entire episode.

Except she has the new cloak. She draws it closer around her and, gathering what is left of her energy, clambers to her feet. She realizes she does not want to lose contact with this man who has been kind to her in her desperate situation, so on painful feet she goes off after him.

4

Her injuries make her progress slow. Still, the one-legged man is not much faster than she herself is, and she could easily catch him if she wanted. But she doesn't; she just wants to know where he is going. She didn't think there were any other settlements for kilometers around, if at all. The lore of her tribe held that they were the only people left outside of the raggedmen who roam the Upground.

And she cannot forget that he is also a raggedman.

They are always dangerous, even ones who share their clothing. Most of the men that wander the wasteland are dangerous; veterans of the Large War, as well as all the minor fighting that followed in the wake of the war—the food riots and water riots, and the furious fighting over the increasingly small tracts of livable land that were left after the cascading climate catastrophes turned the world into a wasteland. As the tribe's Singer—its history keeper—Odile sang about all these troubles.

Driven insane by blood lust and diseased from the effects of lingering radiation and the UV radiation that the thin atmosphere did nothing to mitigate, men were unwelcome in Mae's settlement. The few males that were born into the settlement were expelled as soon as they began showing the aggressive habits of raggedmen. Even without social and environment damage, male children became too violent for the tribe to tolerate.

Sometimes the settlement gave shelter to older men, as long as they were past the age of soldiering and had gotten all the violence of their early years out of their systems. Still, they were never accounted full privileges of participation in the life of the settlement. The settlement was woman's domain.

Up ahead, the man walks on. He goes slow, but seems to be untiring. Not so Mae. The events of the past day and night catch up to her, and when they pass a grove of dead trees sticking stalk-like up from the dry land, she has to stop. She watches the man continue on in his strange one-sided gait.

She can't keep up; she has to let him go without her.

"Thank you," you says to the still air, knowing he will not hear her but needing to voice her gratitude to him for the garment he gave her. This might well save her life.

She finds a depression in the dry landscape among the trees where she might hide. She finishes the last of the water that Cyn left for her.

She wraps herself in the cloak and, broken-hearted at being abandoned and alone without the energy to continue, she lets herself drop into sleep.

In her present despair, she does not care if she ever wakens.

5

But she does.

Again she is pulled out of slumber, this one deep and dreamless. It is screaming that wakes her.

A child's cries.

A girl child, she realizes, as her head quickly clears.

She hears it again. "*No! No!*"

It *is* a child, she thinks. She tries to figure out where the shout is coming from.

"*No!*"

A child!

Mae struggles to her feet and looks around. She sees nothing out of the ordinary, but she is certain a child is yelling.

She hears more screaming, no words now, just inarticulate sounds of raw, animal fear.

Mae hobbles away from the grove where she spent the night and quickly scans the area. A dry plain stretches out.

Rumor has it there used to be very old women in her settlement who had lived around here back when the area was still livable.

Mae thought those stories were outright lies. No one could have been around that long ago and still be living. Every so often, Odile— their tribal Singer, their knowledge-keeper—sings about something that happened during that time, and so some tribe members believed that Odile had been alive back then. But Mae knows that Odile's songs are only lore handed down by other singers over the years, which means Odile wasn't alive back then either.

"*Aaaahh!*"

There it is again . . . and this time she realizes the cry comes from nearby.

Over the rise, she can hear a scuffle. Energized by her need to help, she totters over on aching feet.

When she clears the rise, she sees only the backs of three raggedmen in a gully huddled over a squirming bundle on the ground. Noise rises from the bundle, yelps and squeaks and moans.

The child.

What are these three doing to her?

Mae doesn't stop to think about it—she doesn't *want* to think about what they are doing—but instead shouts as loud as she can with her raspy voice.

"*Stop!*"

The three pause and turn as one to see where the sound comes from, and who would dare to interrupt them.

They are dressed much as the first man who shared his cloak with Mae, but when they turn toward her she can see that their bare faces have been brutalized in the wars and post-war life. One doesn't have a nose, another has the livid lines of scars framing his face from forehead to chin, and the third has only one eye and a mass of inflamed scar tissue on the side of his face where the other eye used to be.

Between them, on the ground, she can see there is a young girl, completely naked, her ragged clothes torn away from her emaciated body. The bones of her shoulders and rib cage are clearly visible under her skin, which shines white in the harsh grim light of day.

Besides being older than the three raggedmen, Mae is also at risk because she has no weapon with which to fight them. She has only her gumption, which will have to do.

One of the girl's attackers rises slowly from the pack and begins to move toward Mae at the top of the rise. It is the raggedman with one eye. Mae sees he has no weapon, either, just his hands, which are bandaged and bloody.

He approaches Mae slowly, sizing her up as easy prey.

When he is almost to her, she swiftly slips her cloak off and swings it around her head and whips it out across his face. A corner of the tatty rough material scrapes across the raggedman's one good eye.

He screams and grabs his face and Mae launches herself at him. She crashes into him and they both career down the dusty slope.

She lands on top of him at the bottom of the gully. She hears the grunt as his breath goes out of him.

She feels something hard at his waist and swiftly reaches down to remove a knife tucked into his pants.

She drives the blade deep into his belly.

His scream is high-pitched and horrible, then abruptly ends when she pulls out the blade and plunges it into chest. She turns with the blade in her hand, but when the other two raggedmen see what she has done to their companion, they run in opposite directions.

The naked girl on the ground curls up, protecting herself. Mae cleans the blade on the rags of the raggedman she has just killed, then sheaths the knife in her waistband. She rises on painful legs and collects the rags that are the girl's clothes and hands them to her.

At that, Mae stands up straight. The world spins and goes dark. She totters and collapses.

6

When Mae opens her eyes, the sun is lower in the sky, but the day is still hot.

How long has she been unconscious?

Hours, it must be. Because the sun never sets, their world is bathed in light constantly. Only the heat varies as the evening draws on. It never abates entirely, but its effect diminishes slightly at night.

She is alone, except for the body of the man she has killed. He lies sprawled in the gully where she left him, dead, like everything else in this world.

The girl has gone.

Mae struggles to her knees with difficulty, then stands and bends over the dead man. Someone—maybe the girl, or maybe there was another raggedman around while she was out—has gone through his clothes. She can tell by the remaining disheveled rags that cover his body. Someone has rifled through his belongings, including the pack he carried. If he had water or food, they are gone now, as is anything else that might have been useful.

The only things left are rags and small objects he must have stowed in his pack, now scattered on the ground. Circular scraps with writing on them that she cannot decipher; ancient papers, brown and shriveled with age, containing faded images of people; stones; ragged feathers that somehow survived the decades since birds went extinct.

Bits and pieces of a former life that held some meaning for him, that remind her of the humanity of the man she was forced to kill, whatever monster he had become.

Not that it made her regret having to extinguish his life. He would not have regretted taking hers. This is the world now.

She sees that he still wears footwear that was not stolen from him. A pair of sandals. She takes those and tries them on. They are too large for her feet, but she is able to fit them over the strips of rags she has been wearing. These will protect her sore feet, as well as provide cushioning between her feet and the rocky ground.

Stiff and sore from her exertions, she continues on in the same direction that the man walked who was looking for her daughter. She thinks the girl she rescued must be the man's daughter. Few youngsters walk around the Upground these days, and none by themselves. How did they get separated? she wonders.

And more importantly, have they gotten back together? Has the girl struck out on her own again, or has she been found by other raggedmen?

Or possibly even the same raggedmen who attacked her, come back to finish what they started?

When she asked the man where his tribe was, he looked silently off into the distance. Now she walks in that direction, hoping he has continued that way.

She is trembling, and remembers she has not eaten since the day before. Hunger and thirst gnaw at her.

Still she walks on.

7

In the morning of the following day, after spending the night beneath a granite overhang, she spots a bundle of rags by the side of a dry river bed in the distance. She approaches carefully. The knife she took off the raggedman the day before is in a pocket of her cloak, and she has also picked up the limb from a dead tree to aid her walking. She has sharpened one end with the knife. Dry and old as the branch is, she doesn't know how sturdy it will be in a fight, but it's better than being visibly defenseless.

She circles the bundle, which she suspects is a body. It is too large to be the body of the girl. At first she thinks it might be the girl's father, but as she draws nearer she realizes the clothing is not the same colors as the father's.

She approaches with the spear point held out in case this is an ambush. She looks around, but sees no place where any companions might hide. She looks into the river bed but sees only sand and the skeletons of long-dead river animals, fish and the bones of what looks to be a larger creature. There are no living predators in this world except for raggedmen.

She comes up beside the bundle of rags and sees it is the body of a man. He lies face-down but his head is turned and she sees the scarring and sores of his face. This was not one of the men who attacked the girl, but another wanderer in the dead, dry land. His body has not attracted the industrious flies and beetles who used to strip the dead because they have all gone extinct; now only the heat does its work on the body, expanding the gasses and melting the skin of the long dead into horrible shapes. Without such distortion, this body is recent, though it still reeks of deadstink.

She uses her spear to turn him over and she picks through his pockets and pack. Nothing in his pockets, but she bends down and cuts the pack away with her knife. She withdraws to a distance from the smell and sits down to see what he carries.

In his pack, she finds a smaller bundle tied with a piece of cloth, and when she opens it she discovers chunks of dried meat. She sniffs. No telling how old this food is, but it doesn't smell rotten. She takes a bite from one chunk.

It has been well-preserved, so the meat is tough but still good.

Her teeth are bad, like most of the members of her settlement, so she takes a bit more off and lets it soften in her mouth before trying to chew it. In this manner, she devours one chunk, then reties the rest and slips it into the pocket of her cloak to save for later.

There is also a container with liquid inside the pack. She sniffs, sticks a finger in and tastes it. Water. A precious find in this world. Probably toxic, as most water is anymore, but she is too thirsty to care. She drinks deeply, but makes herself stop while water is still left in the container. Who knows when she will next find something to drink?

She sits and examines the raggedman's body. He did not appear to die of starvation or dehydration, since he had both water and food; he must have died of disease, or radiation poisoning. It has been years since the wars ended, but the land remains lethal, and who knows what he was exposed to as a soldier.

Mae sits until she feels her strength return, then uses the staff to help get herself back on her feet.

She walks on.

8

On the third day, she is trudging along the sand beside the riverbed when a small stone shoots across her path.

She stops, looks around, and, seeing nothing, continues on her way. Another stone hits her ankle and this time she turns to see where the stone might have come from.

She sees the girl she rescued, peeking over a fallen tree. The girl motions for her to come toward her, then points up ahead.

Mae follows the girl's gesture and sees a group of ten or fifteen raggedmen, sitting in a circle in a clearing of trees and skeletal bushes. They are busy eating and pay no attention to anything but the food in their hands.

Mae scurries over to the fallen tree.

She steps around it and lands in a pile of brush beside the girl. Next to the girl is the man who gave Mae the cloak. He sits with his legs splayed out in front of him.

Before she can say anything, he makes a downward gesture with his hands. Stay low and say nothing, the gesture says.

Mae understands immediately. If the raggedmen discover them, the three will have no chance.

They can't even talk. The man sits with his arm around the girl, protecting her in the depths of the rags of his cloak. The girl eyes Mae, then whispers something to the man. He looks at Mae and gives her a nod of thanks, but holds a finger to his lips so the girl will stay quiet.

The raggedmen sit, eating without speaking, just grunting in satisfaction, for a long time.

Then as a group they rise and leave. Fortunately, their path takes them away from where Mae and the other two are hidden.

Mae and the man and the girl sit for a while longer, until they are certain the raggedmen are gone. Cautiously they stand and stretch their stiff limbs.

The man says, "Thank you." He looks toward the girl. "For saving my daughter." His voice is low. Raggedmen may still remain in the area.

Mae accepts his gratitude with a dip of her head. "I could not do nothing."

"Many would," the father says. "I found her, as you can see."

"Yes," Mae says. "Good."

Now she can tell from the way he looks at the girl that she really is his daughter. His eyes are full of love and sadness.

"We were on our way back to our home," he continues, "when we found that group. You don't often see a group that large."

Mae says nothing. It has been many years since she went out of her own settlement, so she is in no position to comment.

"We're going to continue on our way," the man says. "Do you have anyplace to go?"

"No," Mae admits, without going into the details of how she wound up out her by herself.

"Will you come with us?" the man asks. "You will be welcome."

Mae is overcome by gratitude and relief.

"I will," she says at once.

9

His name is Ross, Mae discovers on their trek. He tells her his daughter's name is Twig. Twig ran away from their settlement, and Ross went out to find her. Entrances and exits are more tightly controlled in Ross's settlement than Mae's, but she found a way out. From what he says, men seem to be a more integrated part of the population than in Mae's.

"Isn't that dangerous?" Mae asks. Her experience of men has been of the same kind as the marauders who attacked Twig—vicious former soldiers who roam the Upground. They are to be avoided, not invited in.

"No," Ross says, "the kind of men who attacked my daughter are not allowed inside. Not all men are like them."

Mae thinks about that as they walk. How can they tell the difference between the good and the bad? She herself thought Ross was a raggedman based on his appearance. What was to stop a raggedman—or a group of them, like the one they just saw—from pretending to be like Ross, until they were allowed into the settlement? Then there would be no stopping them in whatever they wanted to do.

Other questions multiply: What do they eat, how do they live, how do they repopulate? She wonders if his settlement could be an example for the regeneration of her own.

She catches herself. It is not her settlement anymore. She has been banished, and her banishment is permanent.

But it's true; she can't stop thinking of the settlement as her home. It is hard for her to admit that this will have to change.

She waits to ask her questions until she sees the settlement that Ross talks about. Then she will see the answers for herself.

Late in the day, they pass a large body of water that has not yet dried up. The father calls it Lake Winnipeg, surrounded by scores of smaller dips in the dry earth. He says they are the beds of lakes that have long since gone dry.

"Once this was known as the Canadian Shield," he tells Mae. "It was a broad range of granite, with endless kilometers of pine trees where families lived out their lives. Hard to imagine now," he adds.

Mae agrees.

When they are all too tired to continue their traveling, they stop in front of a structure that still has all its walls intact. It is part of a small community, a village in the Before, perhaps, but all the surrounding buildings have been destroyed.

Ross walks around the intact structure, observing it from a distance, then shakes his head.

"Nay. We shouldn't stay here."

"What's wrong?" Mae asks.

"It's perfect," Ross says. "That's the problem. The walls are solid, it looks deserted, there are no other standing structures around. It's the first place raggedmen will look for shelter. We will not be safe here. We have to keep going."

They walk for another klick, then find a cavern—really just a hole in the ground. He crawls in first to make sure it is large enough for the three of them to fit, and that it is empty.

It is. Ross is satisfied this will work.

He helps Twig crawl in first, then Mae, and then he enters. There is no brush around, so he can't block off the entrance. They will have to be vigilant.

"I'll take the first watch," he says. "You two rest."

Twig falls asleep immediately, but sleep will not come for Mae, despite her exhaustion.

While waiting for her body to relax enough to sleep, she chats with Ross to learn more about him.

He and Twig's mother were members of the same tribe. She died giving birth to Twig, he says. Soon after Twig was born, Ross tells Mae, it was clear something was not right with her.

"What was the matter?" Mae asks.

"She was always . . . slow," he says. "Slow to walk, slow to talk. Even now, she doesn't act the way she should."

"She warned me of the band of raggedmen," Mae points out.

"Because I told her to. She would not have thought to do that on her own."

She is just a child, Mae thinks, but does not say.

"All her attempts at escape," he continues, "come about because she does not understand the concept of danger. She doesn't understand so much . . ."

He does not elaborate and Mae does not push him. Few children are born healthy anymore, she reflects. There is no way to care for them, no way to protect them from the thousand diseases and hazards in their world. No way to prepare their mothers for having them safely.

Indeed, few children are born at all anymore in her settlement, healthy or otherwise.

"You say, 'all her attempts,'" Mae says. "She has done this before?"

"Many times."

"Why?"

"As I said. She doesn't understand how dangerous it is out here by herself."

"But why does she want to leave the safety of the settlement?"

He shakes his head sadly. "I don't know what goes on in her mind. And she can't explain it to me, so I'll never understand."

"Still, she is very brave," Mae says, "to go out by herself."

"Brave?" Ross repeats, as though testing the word. "Nay. Foolish."

"Maybe," Mae says, "but still, it takes courage to leave the way she did."

They lie in silence until she says, "The drag-up rate is also high in my tribe."

My former tribe, she silently corrects herself.

"The numbers of dying, you mean?"

"Aye," she says. "Many women used to die in childbirth with us, too. But the births have stopped. We have few young people. We are a tribe of old women, with some old men. Soon all will be gone."

"Our group also," Ross says, "is slowly getting smaller. Do you prohibit men?"

"We do."

Ross nods thoughtfully.

"We don't let in many from the outside," he says. "Most have been with us since birth. There is a process for allowing raggedmen in from the outside."

"It is not safe," Mae points out.

"Sometimes," he agrees. "But by including men, we have a chance to keep our population up. Though many die of the sick, men and women."

Mae knows what he is referring to, and also that "the sick" means a variety of illnesses from radiation, polluted water, cancer from exposure to the sun, and all the major and minor infections that spread unchecked through a group with no medical care.

"What does your tribe do?" Ross asks.

"Do?"

"Aye."

Mae ponders that. Do?

Finally she says, "We struggle to exist. Do you do something different?"

"Aye. We are knowledge-keepers," he says. "Flame-keepers."

"What does that mean?"

"We collect the learning left over from the Before in the form of books. Do you know what learning is?"

"I do," she said. "But not through books. The Singer of our tribe teaches us our learning."

The thought of the Singer—Odile—pains her heart.

"In the books are facts," Ross says. "True information saved through writing."

"Are you a flame-keeper yourself?" she asks.

"We all have roles. Mine is to organize the books that others find. I don't go outside the walls to find books." He looks back at Trig, snoring quietly. "Except when I have to find Twig when she runs away."

Outside the walls, he said.

"You live in the Upground, then?" Mae asks.

"Upground?"

She realizes he does not know what the term means. "Here. On the surface."

"Aye."

"Then how are you protected against the sun and the sick that comes out of the ground?"

"Our home is very large. There are walls and ceilings that protect us from the sun. And floors that protect us from the land. And you?"

She tells him about her settlement—her former settlement—how it is in an abandoned mine, how they have evolved a system of self-government with their Council of Elders, a series of work groups to manage finding food, scavenging supplies, maintaining sanitation, and so on.

"We have done something similar," Ross says. "Though our ruling council is elected by polling proper adults."

"Proper adults?"

"The adults who are compos."

She shakes her head in confusion.

"Many are like Twig," he explains. "Not right from birth. We care for them, but don't allow them to take part in our governance."

She considers that.

"How do you choose your Council of Elders?" he asks

"They are not chosen as your ruling group is. There are nine women in the Council, the nine oldest of the tribe. When one drags up, the next oldest becomes part. The oldest is chief elder, the leader."

She thinks again with an ache of regret about Odile, and how her role in the Council was stolen by Ells. How Ells manipulated the Council's laws to banish Mae when in fact the law did not allow for Ells to seize Odile's position.

"How did you arrive at your system of direction?" Mae asks.

"Through the learning we collect," he says. "From books about the Before. In general, though, our task is not to put the knowledge to use. Our job is to collect knowledge so it's ready for others to put to use when the new times come."

She cannot resist asking, "What others?"

"Those who come after us," he says, "will use the knowledge we save when they must. When the time comes."

They fall silent. New times? There will be none who come after, she thinks. On the dead, dry earth, all the animals and insects have gone extinct; the land is poisoned, so nothing grows; the seas are poisoned, so all the marine life gone. Humans can only be next.

What use is gathering knowledge, Mae wonders, when the race is dying, and there will be no one left to use the knowledge?

And when the knowledge they are keeping is exactly what has brought them here, to the point where life has been destroyed and their own extinction threatens?

They both remain silent as they consider what they have learned about the other.

Without his conversation to keep her awake, Mae drifts into a dreamless sleep.

Until she feels a shake on her shoulder.

She pops awake, her heart pounding.

Ross, waking her for her shift on the watch.

They change places in the cramped, sandy space, and, calming herself, she peeks outside. The night is empty and soundless, except for the occasional crack of a tree branch falling in the distance. The midnight sun bathes the landscape in a soft amber glow that is deadly for all its beauty. Lingering radiation in the air and ground makes being outside dangerous at any hour.

Soon she hears Ross snoring, loud snorts and snuffles. She can only hope no raggedmen are nearby to hear this.

She is reminded of the nights she lay on her mat in her sleeping chamber in her settlement, listening to Odile's gentle snoring. Odile had been training Mae to be a Singer, as Odile is—the history-keeper for the tribe, the sage who connects the tribe to the Beforetime. Odile had been teaching her the story of where they came from, as well as the strategies and forms that she uses to compose her songs.

Unlike the facts written in the books that Ross's tribe collects, Odile's songs are oral, well-suited for transmitting the lore and history of the tribe and the race to people who have lost the skills of reading and writing. Odile was taught by the Singer before her, who in turn was taught by the Singer before her, and so on, back into the past that no one remembers except as part of the songs that the Singers handed down.

Odile.

The memory of Odile's intelligent face makes Mae cry.

What did Odile think when she woke to discover Mae was gone? She will not be allowed to come looking for Mae. But Mae can't imagine that Odile would simply accept her exile and continue on without her. She would have to do something.

To keep herself awake, Mae composes a song in her head. It is a song about her own situation. She imagines singing it to her tribe, especially to Odile, gathered in the elders' chamber as they do to hear Odile's songs.

Listen! Lend me, sisters,   leave to sing my song,
Tribe-chest of the tales   that teach our Before.
This is the sad story   of one of our sisters,
Old she was, an elder,   but able to serve
And tutored in the lore   of her tribe
Preparing to pursue   the purpose of Singer
By Odile the elder   was she ably taught
Till one night when she slept   and a wicked thing happened
Sharply awakened from sleep   was she then
And, bereft of aid or bounty,   nor benefit of food
Nay clothing to keep her safe   from the sun's cutting rays
She was banished, abandoned,   broken her ties
From the tribe whose truth   she trusted
Throughout the long life   she lived in its heart.
Lost from those she loved,   lonely and alone,
Nay place to put   her pitiful head
Till a man she met,   mannered, nay raggedman,
Who gave her a gift   a protective garment
To save her from the sun's   savage looks
And it wasn't long till luck   let Mae repay
His kindness when the man's kin,   his cub,
His daughter in danger   Mae discovered
And truly turned her   from being taken.
Meeting the man again,   they made a pact
To travel together   to the man's tribe
Collectors and keepers of learning   that came to them

Through the dark days   of destruction and wars
Where Mae would be   welcomed, he said,
Being banished as she was   from her own band.
Mae wondered at these words   so worried was she
At having nay home   nay haven of safety.
How this adventure ends   is at present unknown.
And thus truly have I sung   to the tribe this day.

She imagines the reception Odile would give this song. She imagines Odile's face—lined from age, pale from lack of sun and drawn from no adequate diet—smiling her kind smile. The smile that filled Mae with gratitude and happiness.

The smile she will never see again.

She stops herself. She cannot think this way. The thought that she will never see Odile again is too sad to bear. She doesn't know how, but she is certain she and Odile will be together again.

After a while, Ross stirs, and then it is time for him to take his place watching out for the dangers the night may hold.

They try to be silent as they change places, but the disturbance wakes Twig. The girl begins to whine and whimper.

Mae crawls back and wraps her arms around her until the youngster's upset lessens and her breathing deepens. She falls back asleep.

Then Mae lets herself drift again into the relief of slumber.

11

The next morning they have nothing to eat or drink, so when Ross wakes his daughter, she complains of hunger with loud wails.

Mae calms her by holding her and rocking her, then, when she is quiet again, Ross helps Mae and his daughter out of their shelter and back on their journey.

"We will arrive there today," he tells them. "We will have food tonight."

With nothing to sustain them, they do not have the energy to talk. They devote themselves to walking in silence.

Every so often, Ross says, "Not long now."

They have to rest frequently. When Twig's energy fails completely, Ross and Mae take turns carrying her, though Mae herself is dizzy and weak from hunger and fatigue and pain.

Near the end of the day, they slowly make their way up a granite rise and pause at the top. Mae looks down into the bowl of a valley that contains the remnants of a town.

Even from this distance she can tell it has been blasted to pieces. It may have escaped destruction in the Large War—it doesn't bear the tell-tale scorch-marks and pulverized rock from the heat weapons used back then (according to the songs that Odile sang, at any rate)—but the wars over food and water likely did the damage Mae can see. Most buildings are pulled down, great heaps of rubble with only crooked stone chimneys standing. The chasses of burnt-out overturned vehicles and mammoth trucks pushed onto their sides block the streets.

Here and there, ancient unburied corpses of those who dragged up in the wars and unrest remain in the streets, mummified in painful-looking poses by the unremitting heat.

Some structures are still left standing, like scattered teeth in a diseased mouth. Ross points to two long sprawling buildings side-by-side at the far end of what is left of the town.

"There," he says. "Our home."

Home, Mae thinks. Such an old idea. She does not think of her settlement as "home." The word still has associations of comfort, security, safety. These are qualities that passed from her world before she was even born.

And of course, she thinks at once, whatever she calls it, she is not a part of that settlement any longer.

The two structures she views now seem mostly intact. The low buildings are connected by an enclosed passageway at the near end. The walls and roofs have mostly not collapsed, though Mae can see spots where the roof has fallen in in the middle of one of the buildings. Together they appear much larger than her old settlement. From this distance, all the windows seem to have been boarded up.

"Your tribe lives there?" Mae asks. "In those two buildings?"

"Aye."

"What was that place?" she asks.

"It was called a 'processing plant.' At one time, the area around here was very fertile. It was a center for agriculture, especially potatoes. Do you know what those are?"

Mae shakes her head.

"A kind of vegetable." He forms a small orb with his two hands. "Each about this big. Tasty. They grew in the ground, back when the ground could produce food. Those buildings are where the potatoes came to be turned into other products. Other vegetables also came here for processing."

Mae shakes her head at a society that had so many choices for food.

"Follow me," Ross says. He finds a path down the other side of the rise and makes a wide circle around the town.

Wise, Mae thinks. Who can know what dangers might be found in the remaining ruins, among the debris from brick and wood and steel, and the streets where barricades from the food wars are still up, giving possible shelter to raggedmen?

Ross leads them over the cracked pavement that was once a ring road around the town. Though the area is not large, picking their way around the rubble that surrounds it is hard work. It takes them the rest of the day before they arrive at the entrance to the buildings that house Ross's tribe. The sun is low and dim in the evening light.

They stand before a wide, high door at the front of one of the buildings. It is made of corrugated metal with dark, rust-colored streaks. There seem to be no handholds on it, nor any way to open it from the outside. It is not meant to be opened from this side, Mae realizes, only from inside the building.

Ross pounds on the door. It clatters under his fists. Close up, she can see that the rest of the building is made of corrugated metal also, walls and ceilings. There are actually two stories, not one, as she had thought when she looked from a distance.

From the second floor, a deep male voice calls, "Hold!"

Though Ross had warned Mae about the role of men in his tribe, the authoritative sound of a male voice nonetheless unnerves her. In her experience, male voices mean trouble—men's voices bring rape, murder, every other kinds of violence.

She can't tell where it is coming from, until Ross steps back and looks up. "I am Ross, he says. "I bring back my lost daughter, and a visitor."

Mae hears the sounds of men consulting with each other. The voices come from a window on the second level.

A panel swings shut in the window overhead, and the broad door in the front lurches noisily and begins to rise. It seems to wrap around a pole that stretches across the entrance overhead.

The doorway reveals a sentry, a man standing with a staff sharpened on both ends. He is emaciated, but stares grimly at Mae.

He motions the trio to enter.

"I would—" Ross begins to say, but the sentry grabs him by the sleeve of his jacket and pulls him inside.

"Come!" the sentry orders.

When Twig and Mae don't move fast enough for him, he grabs Twig's cloak and pulls her inside. Then he grabs Mae and pulls her in as well.

They are barely inside before the door begins to rattle down. Mae sees they are in a large entrance chamber that is lit only by torches along the walls. There are walls all around the inside, but most of the material on the walls is cracked and some walls are reinforced with wooden planks. It is unbearably hot, hotter even than out in the Upground.

A half-dozen sentries stand behind the one who pulled them inside. All are male and armed with staffs or long broad knives that seem rusty, like the door, in the dim light. They are all dressed like the first sentry, in tattered khaki coats that hang down to the ground.

The main sentry pushes Ross and Twig toward a doorway leading back into the building, but directs Mae into the extension that connects this building with the next one.

"Nay," Ross says, "she stays with me."

The main sentry gives Mae a hard look, then shakes his head and pushes her further into the extension. The sentry bars Ross's way when he tries to follow her.

Another sentry shoves Mae along the hallway until a woman dressed the same as the men steps out of the darkness and grabs her roughly by the upper arm.

"Come," she orders.

Mae resists momentarily, but the woman is terribly strong and squeezes the spare flesh of Mae's arm. The grip is painful, and Mae lets herself be dragged along.

"I'll come back for you," Ross shouts from inside the building. The woman gripping Mae's arm pulls her further into their corridor.

"Where are they taking me?" Mae shouts, but no one can hear her. Ross has already been removed from the entrance hall.

"Where are you taking me?" she asks her guard. Mae receives no reply.

The further they go in the corridor that stretches across to the second building, the harsher the sentry is to Mae, pushing her along and, at one point, grabbing her by the arm and shoving her around a corner so roughly that the older woman falls to the ground.

"Up!" the sentry barks.

"Wait," Mae begs, "I can't move that fast."

The sentry hauls Mae to her feet and shakes her as though she were a doll with no substance, then continues dragging her to an enormous open area. It is larger than any chamber in Mae's settlement.

There is no illumination except for light that comes in from an opening in the roof further down the long chamber. Mae can make out what seem to be scores of mats scattered around on the floor. Some are occupied by people reclining on them, and some are empty. On the other side of the area with mats, dozens of people mill around. Most are younger than Mae, she sees. Raggedmen and women, though women seem to predominate. She sees no children.

Male sentries carrying staffs patrol the area, breaking up fights that pop up or walloping people with their staffs to keep them moving along.

The odor is overwhelming—unwashed bodies, excrement, sickness, and the sour stink of despair. For a chamber housing so many people, it is surprisingly quiet. Through her one good ear, Mae can hear only the soft scraping of feet as people shuffle over the concrete floor, with the occasion sharp cry from someone beaten by the sentries.

Her guard throws Mae to her knees again, and this time Mae sprawls face-first onto the ground. The woman gives Mae a kick to the side, turning her over onto her back. Mae bangs her head on the floor.

The sentry turns and leaves Mae where she fell.

The woman wore no shoes, only rags wrapped around her feet, but the kick was still terribly painful. Mae touches the area tentatively, but even her own gentle fingers makes her grunt in pain. A broken rib, she thinks.

She feels the side of her forehead, which hit the ground when she fell. A painful knot is already rising.

You will be welcomed, Ross had said.

This is not the welcome she expected.

12

Still lying where she was kicked, Mae gazes up at the ceiling. She thinks there may have once been a glass roof over the area further down where the sun shows through, but the panes are all broken. All that is left now is a network of empty frames where the glass used to be. The evening sun casts its amber light on that area. The heat is intense, and the people housed here avoid that space. No one alive remembers when it last rained, so the only element they have to be worried about is the sun. But the sun is dangerous enough.

Mae realizes she is lying among dirty clothes, ancient discarded cans and containers whose contents were long ago devoured, and filth tracked in from outside. She braces herself on her arms and gets her knees under her in preparation for standing. She tries to position her feet, but it's no good; they are too painful; she can't get any support from them, and the new pain in her side won't let her move easily.

Without warning, she feels a pair of arms wrap around her midsection, raising her to her feet. She grunts from the sharp pains, but turns to find a woman who appears slightly younger than she is. The woman releases her and steps back. "All right?" she says.

"Thank you. Yes."

The woman points into the crowd of people. "Come." She leads Mae through the throng to where mats are lined up on the floor. She takes Mae by the hand and guides her to an empty mat. "Now yours," the woman says.

Mae sits with difficulty, and the woman says, "Food?" Mae nods. "Wait," the woman says, and walks away.

In another minute, Mae's new helper returns with a wooden cup filled with water and a bowl of broth. She hands them to Mae and sits cross-legged beside her. She pats Mae's leg and says, "Eat."

Mae drinks both containers down in a few gulps. The broth is bitter but she is starving.

"Better?" the woman asks.

"Better. Thank you again."

The woman smiles, pats herself on her chest. "Jun," she says.

Mae places a hand on her own chest and says, "Mae."

Jun puts her hands together and gives Mae a short bow, which Mae returns.

"What is this place?" Mae asks. She raises her hands, indicating the chamber where they are kept.

The woman waves the question away. "No worry," Jun says. "Find out soon."

Jun holds her hands out and pushes them down twice, as though trying to keep Mae from asking too many questions about their situation.

The woman speaks in the clipped, abbreviated patterns that are typical, like the ones Ross used before he realized Mae could understand more elaborate syntax, which he then began to use. It was the kind of language that Odile and Mae used with each other.

"Rest," Jun says. "Later, talk."

She gets to her feet and gives Mae a pat on the shoulder. Then she disappears into the crowd of people who wander the massive area.

Based on what she knows from her own settlement, Mae guesses this is a large holding pen to keep people until the Ficers are ready to do their work. Her own tribe has something like this, only much smaller, and for raggedmen only. This must be a large settlement, she thinks, if they need to maintain such a huge space to keep this many people.

And where do they all come from, she wonders. There are more people just in this room than are in all of her settlement. (Your *former* settlement, she reminds herself). She has thought her settlement was the only one for many klicks around. For some reason, they have never had contact with this one.

Maybe Ross walked us longer than I suspected, she thinks.

Buoyed slightly by the sustenance Jun has brought her, and by Jun's kindness, Mae lies down on her mat and closes her eyes. Soon the commotion around her fades and, exhausted, in pain, she drops into sleep.

Again, she dreams.

13

In her sleep, she goes back to a time when she was young.

A long time ago.

She was born in the settlement from which she was exiled. She had never lived anywhere else. Her mother had been a Venger at the settlement, taken by a raggedman during one of her scavenging sorties. Back then, there was still food to be found during the scavenging trips. Not much was left from the food wars, but cans and boxes of food, old but still safe to eat, were buried inside the ruins of homes that remained after the riots destroyed most of the structures and all the arable land. By that time, the insects had gone extinct, so the possibilities of growing food had disappeared. Domestic and wild animals across the world were already gone as well.

Children were born into the tribe more often back then, though many women, like her mother, died in childbirth. Mae herself barely survived her first-year bout with measles that left her deaf in her right ear.

She was raised in a chamber of the abandoned nickel mine where the tribe lived. The chamber had been given over to the infants orphaned or abandoned by their parents. As the social order crumbled around the world after the Large War and the many smaller ones as resources disappeared and the populations began to panic, soldiers deserted from their armies and spread out across the country. They did what they were trained to do: kill and suppress dissent. At first they kept to the big cities, but as the cities turned into hellholes (thanks in no small part to the work of the deserters themselves), the ex-soldiers travelled further and further into the heart and soul of the country.

A new kind of society arose: the veterans became the raggedmen terrorizing the Upground, and settlements like Mae's formed, isolated and insulated from the Upground chaos.

Mae now dreams of a time during that dark period. She was still a young child, without family, stable home, consistent food supply, supportive adults, or any imaginable future.

There was, however, a young woman, older than the oldest of the children who were kept in the nursery chamber, who helped care for the children. Her name was Odile. She was an orphan like the others, though she never shared her own history so no one knew if she had been born in the settlement or came from somewhere else.

Mae dreams herself back into the nursery chamber on the day she met Odile. Odile would become the most important person in her life. Mae was only four, but Odile was fifteen. In her dream, Mae sits in the corner of the nursery chamber and can't stop looking at the most beautiful girl she had ever seen. Electricity and gas had not been available for years, so all the rooms were lit only by the uncertain flickering of torches or lanterns. But Odile brings light when she enters the dim area. Or so Mae remembers in her dream.

Odile kneels beside Mae to ask what her name is.

"Mae."

Odile extends a hand and gently brushes Mae's tangled hair away from her face. "Well, Mae, don't worry," Odile says in Mae's dream, her face up close to Mae's, Odile's brown eyes filled with something Mae has never seen . . . concern, maybe, or love (though the little girl in the dream did not even know that word back then). "I'm going to take care of you," Odile continues. "I will never let anything happen to you, Mae. Ever."

With that, Odile smiles, and more light enters the chamber.

Mae looks into Odile's eyes and feels a welter of emotions, and, slowly, reaches out to put her arms around Odile.

Odile responds by hugging Mae back, which no one had ever done before to the orphaned child.

At that moment in her dream, Mae knows they will always be together. She has a flash of dream wisdom that shows her and Odile through the years, always together until they grow old and take their places on the Council of Elders. After Odile becomes the tribe's Singer, she begins to teach Mae to become the next Singer after her.

In her dream, Mae composes a song:

> *Listen! Lend me, sisters,   leave to sing my song,*
> *Tribe-chest of the tales   that teach our before.*
> *The day was destined   when two daughters*
> *From histories hazy   their hearts did join*
> *In the warming world   of wastelands and danger*
> *When futures faded   and friendships helped*
> *To offset the awful coming   of the end of humanity.*

And then, as things do in dreams, the scene switches back to two girls sitting beside each other when they first met as children. Except Odile's face becomes Mae's, and the child Mae in her dream becomes the sleepy, dirt-smudged face of Ross's daughter, Twig.

14

Mae awakens to pain.

Pain in her side, where she was kicked the day before. Pain in her head. Pain in her feet and legs.

People are shuffling around her, and as they pass, their feet nudge her. Accidently—no one aims another kick at her, but they bump her as though she weren't there.

She sits up to see lines forming at two carts where her fellow prisoners—because that's what they all seem to be, under the careful eye of guards—are getting bowls of broth.

It is morning, she sees by the light streaming in through the broken panels of the ceiling.

She gathers herself to stand and join the lines, A passing woman helps her up. Pains up her legs at first, but then the pains ease somewhat as she moves forward to receive her broth.

It is as awful as it was the night before, but she is so hungry that she forces herself to take it in. She needs the nutrition.

When she finishes, she returns the rough wooden bowl to one of the nutrition carts and walks around the area to look for Jun.

When she does not see the woman who helped her last night, Mae returns to her sleeping mat and lies back down.

She sleeps again.

Later in the morning, Ross comes to retrieve her.

He waits until all the sentries are occupied elsewhere and do not have their eyes on her area of the chamber, where Mae is still sleeping.

He gently wakes her and helps her to her feet. "Time to go," he says.

He takes her hand and leads her from the warehouse.

"Easier this way," he explains.

"What do you mean?"

"Avoiding the guards. Better than asking permission."

"What will they do when they find me gone?" she asks.

"No one will even know."

When they are out of the warehouse, Ross asks, "Are you all right?"

"Except for my head and my ribs," Mae says. "And my feet."

Ross looks at the side of her forehead. "How did that happen?"

He reaches out a hand but Mae shies away from it.

"Your head is bruised," he says. "What happened?"

"Part of the welcome you told me I would get."

He frowns, and she immediately regrets being so harsh.

"They did this to you?" he asks.

"Aye."

"So sorry," he says. "I didn't think they would react like that."

Mae shrugs it away. "I am glad to have shelter," she says. Then, "What is that place?" she asks.

Ross hesitates, then says, "Where the strangers stay."

"Strangers?"

"Those who are not part of our group."

"Why?" she asks.

"Why?" he echoes.

"Yes. Why do you keep them all in one place like that? In filth?"

He looks away instead of answering.

"How do they get here?" she persists.

Again, he hesitates before saying, "They find their way. Or," he adds, "they are brought."

Mae doubts many just "find their way." She guesses most are captured and brought, as her tribe does with raggedmen. She knows there are not this many people to be found accidently out wandering the Upground anymore. The Vesters have to go out and look for raggedmen, who rarely find their way to the settlement. And even then, not many are around. They know to keep away from settled areas.

Yet here are raggedmen as well as women, possibly as many as a hundred.

"In my settlement," she says to him, "there are special groups that have to go out and look for raggedmen. Yet you tell me all these people just made their way here?"

Instead of answering, Ross says, "Have you eaten?"

"I had broth with the others this morning."

"Come with me."

He leads her down long corridors to a nutrition chamber. It is another large room, but this one has an intact ceiling overhead. She smells the heavy aroma of meat boiling in large pots.

Her own tribe has long since stopped cooking their food. They discovered means of drying it to preserve it instead, which saves fuel for the torches that light the tunnels. But though she is still hungry, the smell of the boiling meat turns her stomach and she stops. She feels as if she is going vomit, and in fact she bends over and retches but only gags. The vile broth she had earlier stays in her stomach.

Fortunately. She would hate to have to taste it again.

"Are you all right?" he asks when she catches her breath.

She nods.

"Have some food," he says. "You'll feel better."

He shows her where to find more basic bowls carved out of wood, as she used in the large chamber, and a nutrition attendant fills it with a thin watery stew with small pieces of meat from the cooking pots.

"This is better than what you were fed this morning," he assures her.

They seat themselves on the floor and she lifts the bowl to her mouth. She sips. It is oily and tepid. She tastes the meat and finds it underdone, almost raw. The smell is atrocious. It must be spoiled, she thinks.

She can't keep herself from spitting it back into the bowl. Her gorge rises again but she forces herself to keep it down.

He watches her in alarm. "Nay?"

She shakes her head. She puts the bowl on the floor.

"I can't eat this," she says.

"Sorry." He takes the bowl away and returns it to the nutrition station. "I don't have anything else to offer you," he says when he comes back. "This is what we eat."

"Don't worry," Mae says. "But please, tell me more about your strangers."

"I told you about them."

Again, he does not meet her gaze. What is he hiding, she wonders.

"In my settlement," she says, "our Vengers search in the Upground, and when they find raggedmen, they inform the tribe and then the Vesters go out to bring them back. We keep them in a separate area until we are ready to harvest them."

He says nothing, and she continues. "I think you do the same." It is a statement, not a question, so he does not respond.

He does not want to admit it, she realizes. This knowledge-collector, this keeper of the flame, is shamed by the way his people use their strangers.

"We do," he admits, now that he knows that her tribe does something similar.

"Are you ashamed of it?" Mae asks.

He hesitates. "Yes."

"Why?"

He pauses for a few moments before he speaks.

"We keep all the wisdom that is left in the world," he says, "but we are no better than savages. Than animals."

"Savages brought up to this place," she says. "We have always been savages. We are still nothing but savages. But we do what we must to survive, now."

Mae and Ross are both silent.

Rather than pursue it, she asks, "How is your daughter?"

He looks down at his hands clasped in his lap and says nothing. This man is closed tight, she sees.

Finally he says, "She'll be all right." Then, "Would you like to see her?" he asks. He seems relieved to move the subject away from the things he cannot bear to talk about.

"I would," she says.

He stands and helps her up. Her feet are cut and sore from her journey. Her side aches from the kick she received yesterday, and she is woozy from the head injury.

She waits until she is certain she will not collapse, then allows the man to lead her toward his daughter.

15

Ross guides her through a maze of corridors to a section of the building that houses sleeping chambers. The halls are filled with people moving about purposefully, as if they are late for important meetings. Mae sees equal numbers of men and women, all younger than the women in her settlement.

Her *former* settlement, she quickly corrects herself.

Ross stops outside a closed door. "She's in here," he says. "She won't come out."

In this settlement, like her old one, children stay in a different area than their parents. Mae knows this developed because so many children could not be kept with their mothers because the women dragged up while giving birth, or else sickened shortly after birth and dragged up soon after. Other arrangements had to be made for the children, so they were housed together.

Now her tribe is old, so few young women remain. And there are no children. The settlement's future is bleak.

They enter a room where several sleeping mats lie scattered on the floor. Only one is occupied, away in a corner. A small form is curled up on it, head peeking out from under a tattered blanket even though the heat in the room is intense. The blanket moves back and forth as the shape rocks beneath it.

"Twig," Ross says.

The girl ignores him. He gives Mae a woeful look that says, *See what I mean?*

Mae kneels beside her and gently draws the blanket away from the girl's face. Twig's eyes are squeezed shut and she turns her head into the mat, avoiding Mae's gaze. Remembering her dream, Mae reaches out to touch the girl's hair but at the first contact, Twig flinches and shrinks further away from her into the corner.

"Twig," Mae says softly, but the girl does not respond.

"You can see how she is," Ross says.

Mae nods. "When she left the settlement, how did you discover she was gone?"

"I came to bring her to first feeding, as I always do. When I saw she was not here, I looked around both buildings for her, and when I didn't find her, I suspected she might have slipped out."

"Do you always go looking for her when she escapes?"

"Aye."

Mae lays a gentle hand on Twig's shoulder, but the girl makes an odd, high noise and Mae withdraws her hand at once.

So terrified, Mae thinks.

Perhaps a monster of Twig's own mind forces her to keep running away?

Or, more likely a living, breathing monster, Mae suspects. She cannot bring herself to leave her distrust of men behind. She wonders if Twig left because of something one—or more—of the men was doing to her. Especially if she stays here with other children, away from her father's supervision; she is vulnerable.

She is young, but she is a female. And therefore prey for men.

"We should let her rest," Ross says. "Usually when I bring her back after one of these episodes, she has to sleep. And then she'll stay. At least for a while."

Mae looks down at the girl. Her face is dirty. She has not been washed off since she got back the night before. "Do you have hygiene stations?" she asks Ross.

He gives her a quizzical look and she says, "How do you keep yourselves clean?"

"Not with water. Water is too precious to use for personal washing. We have to use it for drinking and food preparation. Come," he says, as though anxious again to change the subject (so much this man refuses to talk about, she thinks), "Let's leave her for now. I'll show you the library. Where I do my work."

He helps Mae to her feet, and leads her to a large area in the middle of the building. It is as big as the chamber where the strangers are kept. Head-high shelves line the walls and fill the center of the room. There are only narrow aisles between the shelves. The place smells of must and mildew and rotting paper.

"These are our books," he says with pride.

"Books," she murmurs.

The shelves are crammed with them, rectangles of every size, shape, and color—reds, greens, and browns, primarily, but also brighter colors from wrappers around them.

Ross picks up an object from one of the stacks. "You know about books?" he asks her.

"One of the Vengers in my tribe brought one back. She was told about it by a man she met on a scavenging."

"He was probably one of our group," Ross says. "Did she say his name?"

"No."

"We have those whose task it is to go out and find books for our library. They travel all over."

Ash, the Vester who told the tribe about the man with a book, also told the group that the man was dragged up by other marauding raggedmen.

"He did not survive," Mae says.

Ross accepts the news with a single bob of his head. "Thank you for telling me. I'll find out who that was and announce it. Sometimes," he says, "they are gone for weeks at a time. They range everywhere, so it's hard to say when one of them goes but never returns."

He hands the book to her.

It is old—maybe the oldest thing she has ever seen, older than the book Ash brought back—and the cover smells of dry rot. When she opens it, she sees orderly designs in rows on the delicate pages. She knows the designs are called "writing," but she cannot decipher them. She knows that Odile can. She learned before the skill was lost.

In fact, there was a dispute in the Council of Elders in her tribe about the story of the book that Ash brought back. Odile thought the book was important because of what they could all learn from it. But another elder, called Ells, argued against it. Ells said because a man told Ash about the book, it was evil by association and would do no good for the tribe. Mae herself argued for it strongly along with Odile, but the other elders agreed with Ells.

It was this dispute that led to Mae's banishment as part of Ells's attempt to wrest the chief elder's position away from Odile and take it for herself. The chief elder by tradition is the oldest woman in the tribe, but she still must be approved by the Council. As one of Odile's strongest supporters, Mae had to be gotten out of the way before Ells could work her plan to usurp the role.

Mae also suspects her banishment was meant to terrorize Odile, as well.

"These are very valuable," Ross says.

"I know," she replies, and gives the book back to him.

"The learning of the old world is contained in this room. The learning in these books must not be lost forever."

She begins to examine the contents of the rest of the shelves. There are books of all sizes—books as small as Mae's hand, and books almost as large as a sleeping mat. She takes one book down that contains pictures of events that must have happened centuries ago, including pictures of a lush green world seen from the air. Both the fertility of the old world and the high, wide perspectives of the pictures seem magical.

"Those are called *photographs*," Ross says. "They duplicated pictures of the world on paper. There were special machines to make them and turn them into books."

This is the Before world, she thinks as she pages through the photographs. What has been lost. Or thrown away, to be more accurate. This is the world that Odile sings about in her songs of the tribe's history.

It is almost impossible for Mae to believe that her dead, dry world once looked like this.

Ross says, "We have taken it on ourselves to preserve the knowledge of the past. Once these were everywhere," he says, sweeping his hand around the chamber. "Everyone could read them. Everyone could get them. These were how knowledge and wisdom were preserved and handed down from generation to generation. Almost all of them are gone now. They were destroyed in the food riots when the educated elites were thought to be hoarding food. The starving people destroyed the homes of the elite, and burned every repository of books in homes, libraries, schools . . . Along with anyone with an education who had the bad luck to come into contact with the mobs. But some books survived, along with a small number of educated people who had gone into hiding from the mobs. We try to save them, too, along with the knowledge of the past."

"And your job is to arrange the books here? In the library?"

"Aye."

"How do you organize them? Do you have to read them to see where they should go?"

"I can't read," Ross admits.

"You can't?"

"Nay. The librarians read the books and tell me where to put them."

Mae considers that.

"How can you work in this place and not be able to read what you have collected?"

"My task is not to read," he says. "My task is to arrange."

"Do many people here read?"

"Some do. The ones who search for books. The librarians. The educated people who hide here. Our children are also taught to read."

"But they didn't teach you, too?"

"Oh aye. They tried. But I couldn't learn. Maybe I am slow, too. Like Twig."

He gazes sadly at the books, whose contents would forever be a mystery to him, then looks back at Mae with a wan smile.

She walks around more of the shelves. On some are book filled mostly with pages and pages of writing. Others contain the pictures Ross called *photographs*, both black and white and in color, showing men and women walking around, talking and laughing in fine clothes, doing things in a world that no longer exists except as the lore in the Singer's songs. People are shown using large and complicated machines that traveled over the ground, flew in the air, and balanced on top of bodies of water. In her early days, she occasionally saw what was left of some of these when she would walk around when she was a Venger.

Now, on her way to this settlement, she still saw a few of these. They have been scavenged or destroyed in the intervening years, so there isn't much left of them.

But this is the world we came from, Mae marvels again. The world we killed, and that killed us. And will continue to kill us until there is nothing left over the entire dead earth.

She opens more books and discovers pictures of creatures with long, graceful necks and perfectly groomed coats in every color. Again, these are all gone. They exist only now in these books that Ross and people like him are driven to find and rescue from the debris their ancestors created.

When the human world dies out eventually, like the animal and vegetable worlds, what will be the sense of keeping all of these books? No one will ever see them. Few enough people understand them as it is, Mae knows.

She glances at Ross and sees he, too, is lost in thought. From the look on his face, though, she can tell that he is not thinking about what happens when no one is around anymore to read these books and learn this knowledge. Nay, the expression he wears tells Mae he is thinking about what a wonderful thing it is that they have saved all this accumulated learning of the human race.

Even if he doesn't understand any of it.

A sudden commotion comes from elsewhere in the building. The rumble of running feet and the sounds of cries of alarm. A shout is relayed through the building and makes its way back to them.

Mae can't make out what it says, but the meaning is clear from the look on Ross's face.

He is wide-eyed in fear.

16

After a few moments, Ross unfreezes and starts limping away from her toward the door.

"Wait here," he tells Mae. He holds out a hand as though pinning her to the spot.

"What is going on?"

"Something is happening," he says. "Something bad."

He pauses at the door and turns back to her. "Please take care of Twig," he says, and then is gone.

"Wait," Mae says. She follows him, but he plunges into a rush of men and women streaming toward the front of the building and she immediately loses sight of him in the crowd.

Then a group comes running in the opposite direction, from the front toward the back. They look terrified. Mae tries to stop a few to ask what is happening, but they will not pause. They shake her off and continue hurrying on their way.

She steps in front of a woman racing down the hallway, and says, "What is happening?"

The woman cries, "Attack," and then pushes away from Mae and keeps running past her.

Mae fights through the confusion to the front of the building, where she can't see anything because the front windows are all blockaded and there is a large cluster of people obstructing her view. The men are all shouting directions at each other and no one is paying attention to anyone else.

From outside come the deep voices of men yelling in a rising swell, and she hears a pounding that shakes the building.

Raggedmen outside must be attacking the settlement, she realizes.

She makes her way on painful feet up a stairway to the second level, where all the windows are not blocked out. The guards who were up here the day before are gone, no doubt now part of the chaotic scene below. She swings open a panel in front of one of the windows and gazes down.

From her vantage point, she sees a legion of raggedmen outside, maybe a hundred. They are screaming and whooping and wielding staffs and branches from the dead trees that are everywhere.

And they are pushing forward toward the big entrance door.

The pounding, she sees, is a great tree trunk that a dozen raggedmen are using to batter the front door where she and Ross entered. For a short while the door resists, but then she hears a tremendous screech of metal. As she watches from the second-floor window, the tree disappears inside down below, as though the building has eaten it. With her one good ear, she hears that the raggedmen have broken through the door.

The shouting gets louder.

Mae looks around for a weapon so she can join this battle, or at least try to protect herself, but sees nothing she could use. She returns to the staircase as fast as her painful legs will allow her and pauses midway down to see a vicious battle between going on the residents of the settlement and the raggedmen invaders.

The raggedmen are pouring through the opening they have punched in the metal front door. The settlement people are massed around the door trying to push them back, but the raggedmen seem driven by a crazed anger that makes them hard to resist repel.

What could they possibly want here to justify such fury, Mae wonders. There's nothing here of value except books, and she is certain none of the invaders can even read.

This must be what the food riots were like, she thinks. Insane mobs bent on destruction for its own sake.

In the midst of the fight, she sees Ross struggling with a raggedman. They go at each other with staffs, lunging and parrying and taking roundhouse swings with their weapons.

Mae watches as Ross holds his own with his enemy, but finally Ross is no match for the hatred that blazes out of the raggedman's eyes and powers his attack. The raggedman knocks Ross's artificial leg out from under him with a sharp blow. Off balance, Ross falls to the ground and, to Mae's horror, before Ross can roll out of the way the raggedman drives his sharpened staff down through the center of Ross's chest.

Twig's father jerks, spasms, opens his mouth to let out a cry that is lost in the clamor, then lies motionless, pinned to the ground. Mae knows he will not rise again.

With their guards gone to join the battle against the invaders, the strangers who were kept in the other building are now escaping into this building. Like a single organism, they flow through the hallway between the structures and then toward the back, away from the fight.

For a moment, Mae considers picking up a staff and joining the fight, but as she sees the raggedmen viciously overcoming the defenders, she makes a different decision.

She lets herself be pushed along with those running into the back of the building. She makes her way to Twig's room, where the girl is still huddled under her blanket, trembling now.

Mae tugs the blanket away and despite the pains in her body, she pulls Twig up onto her feet. Even under the dirt on her face, Mae can tell the girl is pale with fear.

"Come," Mae orders, "we have to go."

Twig makes a noise that sounds like, "Nay!"

"Aye!"

The girl pulls away from Mae and shrinks into the corner against the wall. She folds her hands into fists and puts them up to each side of her head and makes an eerie ululation that raises the hairs on the back of Mae's neck and sends an icy chill down her spine.

This must be what her father meant, Mae realizes. She's not well.

The girl stops making the sound and glares at Mae; her eyes burn with hatred and panic. The older woman forces herself to be calm and says, "You have to come with me," quietly but loudly enough to make herself heard above the commotion outside Twig's room. "We are in danger. We have to leave."

"Father," the girl hisses.

Knowing she can't tell the girl the truth if she wants a chance of saving her, Mae says, "Come with me and we'll find him."

"Nay!"

Twig begins the ululation again and Mae steps forward and puts her arms around the girl. She holds her tightly and at first Twig tries to extract herself by squirming and wiggling, but Mae holds on and the girl's squirming subsides and she grows quiet, just as she did on the trek here when Mae would embrace her.

"Come with me," Mae whispers in Twig's ear. With an arm around Twig's shoulders, Mae guides her, now docile, out of the room. The halls are chaotic, but more people are running away from the front now than toward it. Mae lets the stream of people carry them along, still holding Twig close.

The crowd seems to know where it is going. It flows toward a back entrance. Mae feels Twig getting worked up again, so she separates them from the flow and leans against a wall, holding Twig close.

That calms the girl down, and Mae is about to rejoin the group exiting when the flow of people reverses itself and Mae sees a trio of raggedmen burst through the back entrance. One raggedman has a sharpened staff which he is using to stab everyone within reach. Another raggedman has a long broad knife and is swinging it wildly, cutting down people on all sides of him.

Mae pulls Twig away from the carnage and down a hallway and around a corner. Her feet are so painful she doesn't know if she can go on, but her main task now is saving this girl from the slaughter so she tries not to think about the torment that is hobbling her.

The settlement is under siege from the front and the back. Mae goes with Twig down a corridor that feels like it might be at one side of the building. They look inside every room, but find no means of exit; every window is blocked.

Finally they make their way back to the library. From one end of the hallway, Mae hears a savage growl. She turns to see a raggedman making his way toward them, his face twisted in rage.

She ducks with Twig inside the library and slams the door behind them. They race around the maze of shelves, trying to put distance between themselves and the raggedman who might be following.

Mae spots a door on an outside wall. She tries it, but it is locked. And probably nailed shut too, she thinks angrily. She tries to shoulder it open, but the door won't budge.

She looks it over quickly, and discovers catches hidden at the top and bottom. She throws the levers on the catches and tries the door again.

It opens.

17

Mae peeks outside. She was right, they are on one side of the long building. She sees no raggedmen, nor any activity at all nearby. All the action is at either end of the building. The invading raggedmen must not have found the other entrances.

She wraps an arm around Twig's shoulders, opens the door all the way, and steps out into the dry air. It seems cool out, compared with the oven inside.

When she realizes what is happening, Twig begins her ululation again. She stops to shout for her father, then resumes the weird and disquieting sound.

The noise Twig is making is lost in the sounds of the battles from the front and back. Mae takes Twig by the hand and leads her out to a stone wall parallel to the building. The wall has crumbled so all that remains comes up to Mae's knees. She pulls Twig down and hunkers beside her.

Twig is thrashing and calling for her father. The commotion from the fights around the building seems to be feeding her anxiety.

They are certainly feeding mine, Mae thinks.

From where they are hiding, Mae can see very little of what is happening in the front. But she can see a line of raggedmen appear who run toward the side door that Mae and Twig just exited. They are shouting and waving their spears and long knives.

As Mae watches, they discover the door she has just exited from, and they rush through it. If Mae had delayed their escape by even a minute, she would have run right into them. She hears screams coming from inside the building, not only full-throated roars from the raggedmen but also wails of terror from the residents of the settlement.

Mae takes Twig by the arm and together they creep along the wall, keeping out of sight below the top stones. They head away from the front of the building, but at one point Mae stops and peeks over the wall. She sees a dozen raggedmen appear and converge on a back entrance. They enter and shortly another group of raggedmen emerge, pulling men and women outside and driving their pointed stakes into their prisoners and slashing at them with their long blades.

The residents of this settlement are being slaughtered.

Among those being led out of the building, Mae recognizes Jun, who helped her the day before. A thought—I must save her—flashes across Mae's mind but as she watches, a raggedman slashes at Jun with his blade again and again until she falls over and her body lies bloody on the ground.

This is hopeless, Mae realizes. None of them will survive. If she and Twig have any chance, they have to get as far away as they can from all this.

Now she sees smoke billowing from the side door they had exited through. That was the library; the only things that can burn in that room are the books.

They are setting fire to the books.

The accumulated knowledge of the ages that Ross was so proud of maintaining . . . it's all going up in flames.

Mae sees orange tongues of fire appear in the doorway, as though the fire is tasting the air.

Why are they doing this, she wonders again. These raggedmen cannot read any more than she herself can. Or even Ross himself, for that matter.

They must be setting the books on fire for no other reason than to destroy what is left of the learning of this world, she thinks. They are burning the books because they can. Just like the mobs who destroyed the educated people in the old days and razed the schools to the ground.

Just like the mob of raggedmen is doing now, in spasms of insane fury at any suggestion of civilization or order. Even now it continues, the urge to destroy whatever meagre civilization exists.

Simply because they can.

She turns from the scene and, pulling Twig along, heads away from the stone wall toward the forest of dead trees that lies beyond the settlement. She moves as quickly as she can on her painful feet as she urges Twig along. She keeps an eye on the building behind them to make sure no one is chasing them.

Every step takes them further away from the massacre.

Mae keeps moving with Twig until they are out of sight of the building and the remains of the town. And they are out of earshot of the terrible screams that come from the extermination of the people in the settlement, residents and strangers alike.

They come to a hillock and slide down a sandy ridge. At the bottom, Mae lets go of Twig's hand and the girl immediately folds into a fetal position on the ground, where she lies, whimpering, while Mae sits and catches her breath. She badly needs to rest.

They both remain where they have fallen. Mae is aware that the full glaring sun bears down on them in the gully. In the haste of their escape, she had brought no protections for them against the sun and its dangerous rays.

Twig lies there in the flimsy cloak she was wearing when Mae took her from her sleeping mat. Mae takes off the cloak that Ross had given her and covers Twig with it from head to foot. The girl, at least, will be safer from the sun.

By the time Mae has recovered her breath, Twig has stopped whimpering. Maybe we can continue, Mae thinks.

Before she can move, a spray of sand bursts over the ridge and something drops heavily down on top of them.

18

Defenseless, Mae can only watch as something—no, it's someone!—rolls to a stop and sits up.

Mae realizes the intruder is another woman, younger than she is but older than Twig. The woman rolls out of her fall in an attack posture, holding out a staff like the ones the raggedmen use. She points it at Mae.

Is she one of them?

After a moment, when Mae does not attack her, the woman brushes sand out of her short hair and blinks it out of her eyes. She is dark complected, with green eyes set deep into a face that despite her youth is lined and cracked from exposure to the Upground.

The woman looks at Mae, then at Twig. Mae realizes she has seen her before. She was one of the prisoners in the warehouse where she herself was taken after her arrival. Mae remembers the woman because she spent all her time pacing around the chamber.

The woman looks around. "Alone?" she now asks. Her voice is deep and gravelly.

Mae nods. "From there?" she asks. She points back toward the line of smoke from the burning building, which is all they can see now.

"Aye."

"Prisoner?" Mae asks. She adopts the terse, telegraphic speech this young woman uses.

The stranger gives a peculiar cocked twitch of her head that Mae realizes is a nod. "Escape," she says.

"During attack?" Mae asks.

Another cocked nod.

"Mae," Mae says, and pats her chest. She points to the girl. "Twig."

"Anya," the woman says.

Mae repeats the name, then asks, "Where from?"

Anya considers that for a few moments, then gives a wry smile. "Nowhere," she says.

"Nay have home? Nay tribe?"

Anya shakes her head. "Wander, me."

"How you survive?" Mae asks.

Anya shrugs. How does anyone survive in these times?

The same way the raggedmen did? Mae wonders. By preying on others?

Mae glances at the staff Anya is still holding, and decides to ask if she is connected with the raggedmen somehow. Better to know who she is and what kind of threat she may pose.

"Live with raggedmen?" Mae asks.

"Nay," Anya says. "Stay away, raggedmen."

She notices Mae eyeing her staff, and lowers it. "Picked up," Anya says, indicating the staff. "From dead raggedman."

Mae says nothing at this bit of information. Then she asks, "Nay with raggedmen, why live Upground?"

"'Upground'?"

Mae holds her hands out. "This. Out here. Where you wander."

"Stayed in settlements. Nay like."

Mae says, "Mmm." Anya says nothing more about that.

"Stay there," she continues. She points back toward the ruined town. "Till caught. Then there." Now she indicates the smoke rising from the building where they all escaped from.

"I saw you there," Mae says.

"You caught, too?"

"Aye," Mae says.

Anya gives Mae a long look. "Kept for . . ." Anya says, and she doesn't need to say any more. Mae understands that she was kept in the warehouse to be sacrificed and used as food when her time came, just as Mae briefly was.

Anya lifts her chin toward Twig. "Your?"

"Nay."

"Gran?"

Mae shakes her head. "Nay relation," she says.

"Where father?"

At the sound of the word, Twig picks her head up and looks at Anya.

Anya and Mae exchange a look. Mae gives her head a small shake, and Anya raises her chin in return. The women understand each other: Twig's father must not be spoken of.

Anya looks on the ground around Mae and Twig. "Nay weapon?" she asks.

"Nay."

"How fight?"

Mae sighs. "Too old to fight," she says.

"Nay," Anya says. "Must fight. Or die," she adds, matter-of-factly.

Before Mae can say anything more, Anya rises and after making sure no one is around, she climbs out of the gully where they are hiding and goes into a stand of trees. She tugs on dead limbs until she finds one that snaps off. She hefts it and examines both ends.

She returns with it to Mae. "Knife?" she asks Mae.

"Nay," Mae says. She and Twig fled so quickly she had no time to think of taking anything.

Anya nods and searches on the ground till she finds a stone. Slowly she scrapes one end of the tree limb over the rough surface of the stone, turning it until she is satisfied it is sharpened to a point. Then she turns the limb around and does the same with the other end.

She tests the points and gives the shaft to Mae. "Weapon," Anya says.

"Good," Mae says. "Thank you." She does not know how she can possibly use this, but understands Anya is trying to help.

Anya sits back down beside Mae.

"What will you do now?" Mae asks.

"Away, me," Anya says. "Far. You?"

That's a good question, Mae thinks. Where to go? She shakes her head.

Mae looks at Twig, still in her fetal position. How can she travel—where can she travel—with the young one in such condition?

Anya sits watching her calmly, waiting for her answer.

Mae feels compelled to say something. What makes the most sense for her and the girl?

The answer is obvious. "I could go back to my settlement with Twig," she offers.

It's the only security she knows, even if they have banished her. She can't just wander the Upground with Twig. They will never survive.

But then she gives her head a short, involuntary shake as she realizes the settlement will not take her back.

Alert to the quick movement, Anya says, "What?"

"Nothing."

Anya rejects that with a shake of her own head. "Tell," she insists.

"I had trouble there," Mae says. "They may not take me back. But they will take Twig. They have to."

Anya continues to watch, unpersuaded.

But it's not her problem, Mae thinks. It's mine. And this little girl's.

Finally Anya collects her staff and stands. "Luck," she says.

"Thank you."

"I go, me."

"Wait," Mae says, before she actually thinks about it. "Anya. Come with us."

Anya shakes her head without even giving the idea a second's thought.

"You will be welcome," Mae says, aware she is echoing what Ross said to her, and remembering the harsh introduction she actually received. But her tribe would welcome both Twig and Anya, she insists to herself, despite Twig's difficulties.

And despite Mae's presence.

Her tribe is dying out; these young members would be very welcome.

Or they would have been in the version of her tribe that Mae knew. Is she really so sure now, considering what her tribe seemed to be turning into?

In any event, three women would be safer traveling together than two. Especially since Anya seems to Mae to be a warrior. She would have to be, to survive on her own.

"Come with us," Mae says again. "At least as far as the settlement. Then you can go any way you wish. Or stay there," Mae adds, "if you want."

"Nay stay. Nay settlement, me."

"Then just help us get there. You see how Twig is. What shape I'm in. I don't think we can make it there on our own. Please help us."

Anya considers it for a few long moments, then says, "Aye. Get you there. Then go."

"Thank you," Mae says.

"Now nay stay here," Anya says. "Go. Now." She points the tip of her staff back toward the building they came from, the column of smoke now thick billows. "Too danger."

Mae agrees and Anya helps her up, and together they coax Twig to her feet. Mae tries to take Twig by the hand, but the girl refuses to budge. Anya grabs her up and hoists her over her shoulder and strides off.

Mae has to hurry to keep up.

When they have walked far enough to put distance between themselves and the burning library, Anya stops and sets Twig down gently. The three seat themselves in the skimpy shade of a massive pine.

"Where settlement?" Anya asks Mae.

Who can only search the empty landscape helplessly. She is too confused to know, too upset, too uncertain of how they came, or which direction is even north.

Anya looks around and says, "Rest night here."

"Aye," Mae says with relief, aware of how tired she is.

While Mae and Twig sit and watch, Anya collects fallen tree limbs and constructs a lean-to around Mae and Twig.

"Nay see," she tells them. And when she is through, the three women are indeed out of sight behind the makeshift wall of branches leaning against the pine.

They will alternate keeping watch, Mae and Anya decide. Mae volunteers for the first shift so Anya can rest. She lets Anya sleep, and then when Anya wakes, Mae sleeps.

At some point during the night, Mae wakes to find Anya is gone from their shelter. Mae steps outside, but the Upgrounder is nowhere in sight in the midnight sunlight.

She's gone, Mae realizes sadly. Even the possibility of staying in one place must have frightened her.

Mae silently wishes her well. She had begun to count on Anya's help and protection, but she tells herself they will find a way back to her settlement somehow.

She tries to stay awake on watch by herself for the rest of the night.

But she is too tired and dozes off.

19

Mae wakes from a dreamless sleep to the smell of meat roasting. She jerks upright and looks out of the shelter.

She sees Anya tending a small fire, turning strips of meat on sticks. The burning wood is fragrant, comforting as it snaps and pops.

Anya hands a skewer to Mae. "Eat," she says.

"Where did you get these?" Mae asks.

Anya makes a vague gesture behind her. "There."

Mae looks around and sees nothing but the dead landscape. She decides not to press it. Best not to ask.

Instead she says, "The fire will draw raggedmen?"

"Nay," Anya says with certainty, and continues turning the meat, thick chunks that drip fat hissing into the fire.

Though remembering how the smell of meat in the nutrition chamber the day before turned her stomach, Mae is too hungry to refuse. She takes a tentative bite from a chunk on the skewer.

She expects to be disgusted, but to her surprise the meat is savory and tender—so different from the boiled meat at Twig's settlement.

Anya watches her. Mae holds up the skewer and says, "Good."

"Aye," Anya says. "Wood give flavor."

Mae takes another small bite. She can taste the smoky tang imparted by the sweet-smelling logs Anya uses to cook the food.

When Mae eats her portion, she wakes Twig, who at first groggily refuses the offer of food, then gobbles down the meal gratefully.

Anya roasts more than they can eat now and wraps the rest in a pack she has produced. Mae is certain she didn't have that with her the day before; she suspects it came from the same source as the meat, but doesn't mention it.

Anya covers the fire with sand to extinguish it, then approaches Mae with a bowl formed of a natural depression in a small rock. In it is something grey and thick.

"For you," Anya says.

It smells vile. "I can't possibly eat this," she says.

For the first time, Anya smiles, a wry, crooked grin. Like everyone else in this world, she is missing teeth, but her smile brightens her face.

"Nay for eat," she says. She sets the rock down and slips the sandals from Mae's aching feet and unwraps the bloody rags. She dips two fingers into the bowl. Her fingers bring out an oozing jelly, which she gently rubs onto Mae's cuts and scrapes. At first the unguent stings, but then it feels cool and eases the pain.

"Where did you get that?" Mae asks her. She has heard that people made medication from plants in the Before. But there have not been plants for years; everything now is dusty brown or red, with no living vegetation anywhere.

"I made," Anya says.

"From what?"

"Bones, stalks of plants, roots. Mixed with drippings from food."

"How did you—" Mae begins, but the scowl on Anya's face glaring up at her quiets her before she can say another word. Too many questions. Too much talking.

When she is finished, Anya rewraps Mae's feet with different cloths and says, "Soak in. Stop for tonight, do again."

"Thank you," Mae says. Anya accepts the gratitude with one of her cocked nods, which Mae now understands is a characteristic gesture.

Before she rises, Anya lifts Mae's pants legs and rubs the salve along the cuts and scrapes.

Her belly full and the pains in her feet eased, impressed again at Anya's skills, Mae leans back on the ground. She holds a hand in front of her face to block the sun, and before long she dozes.

When she wakes, she sees Anya squatting on her heels in front of her, looking out across the rolling landscape. Mae looks around but doesn't see Twig.

When Anya notices Mae is awake and searching, she points silently to where Twig is scuffling through the sand a few meters away, her eyes on the ground.

"All fine," Anya says. "Better?" she asks. She indicates Mae's feet.

"Yes. Thank you for what you did."

A cocked nod.

"So," Anya says. "Where settlement?"

Mae shakes the sleep from her head. "Not sure," she admits, realizing she really has no idea which way to go.

"How you come?" Anya asks.

Mae searches for a way to explain, but can't find the words.

Anya says, "In morning, sun on——?" Here she points over her left shoulder, then ever her right.

Mae concentrates. She started out from her settlement in the early morning . . . which side was the sun on as it rose?

She tries to visualize it. But she was so upset—she had been torn from her tribe, beaten, banished—

"Left side," she says. "The sun was on my left when it rose that first day." She raises her left hand.

"Other days?" Anya asks.

"Left, too."

Anya nods. Problem solved. If the sun was on her left, Mae walked south. So now they need to walk with the sun on their right if they are to retrace their steps back to the settlement.

They start out. Even Twig is in a better mood than she has been. Rested, with food in their bellies and confidence in their guide, Mae feels better about their chances of finding—and gaining entrance to—her former home.

At the least, she thinks, they might will let in her companions, even if they send her away.

Or decide to kill her.

20

At the end of the second day of walking, Mae can no long pretend she can keep going on her sore feet, despite the relief from Anya's salve. She has to stop.

"Sorry," Mae says. "Nay go further."

She finds a tree to lean her back against to take weight off her feet, and despite her efforts to stay upright, she slides down to the ground. She lands with a jolt that goes up her spine and makes her wince.

She stretches her legs out. With the pressure of her weight gone, her legs immediately feel better but the sharp aches in her feet persist.

Still, she feels badly that she is slowing them down.

When Twig sees Mae on the ground, she lets herself drop right where she is standing. She is also tired, Mae knows, though Anya carried her for part of the day.

Twig begins drawing designs in the sand with her fingers.

"All need rest," Anya says. "Stay here tonight."

Anya searches around but cannot find a cavern or secluded depression in the ground, nor any brush for building a shelter in the gently rolling land. Instead, she finds a dead tree with a broad, low-hanging branch where they can be out of reach of any raggedmen. After first making sure it is sturdy enough, Anya helps Mae to her feet and together they lift Twig up to the branch. Then Anya helps Mae up, and shinnies up herself.

Anya is tough and strong, Mae notices again, as well as resourceful. A life spent in the Upground will do that. Mae believes

Anya is stronger than any of the men they will encounter. It cheers her; with Anya's help, they will make it safely back to the underground settlement.

There is ample room for the three of them on the wide limb, but Anya ties Twig to the branch with Twig's coat so she won't fall off. At first, when Anya puts her hands on Twig, Twig raises her ululation, but both Mae and Anya calm her and she quiets down. Both women hope her sound did not echo out into the bare valley that surrounds them.

"You sleep first," Anya tells Mae. "Watch, me."

Mae agrees at once. She is exhausted and her feet are terribly sore. Anya helps Mae tie herself to the branch, and Mae drops off to sleep immediately.

And dreams.

She dreams of one of Odile's songs from long ago, a meandering, enchanting composition, the first song she ever heard Odile sing. A young Mae sways to its rhythms in her dream, as the subject matter horrifies and fascinates her.

> *"Listen! Lend me, sisters,   leave to sing my song,*
> *Tribe-chest of the tales   that teach our Before.*
> *This story of the sorrows   that struck our elders*
> *A tale of wars and woes   and wasting illness*
> *That brought us, bereft,   to this heartbroken life.*

Odile sits on the Singer's mat in the Council of Elders' chamber. Her head is back, her eyes are closed, and her mouth hangs agape as the words seem to come from some place other than her own body in a voice that is strong and clear. The young dream-Mae does not understand every word in the song, but she comes to understand that the song is about the long-past history of their tribe and the race.

> *The Large War waged   for years, no winners,*
> *Starting small   across the world*
> *Then spreading to the ends   of every nation,*

86

One insane, stupid leader   sparking it all,
Raging everywhere, red-hot,   raining flames
Across the earth   ablaze and aglow
With deadly, dangerous   damage to all,
Poisoning the people,   plants, animals,
All perished in pain   producing the world
Left to us to live in   a lost eden
Destroyed: dry earth,   dead earth,
A worried world   in which
Man is fleeting, woman fleeting   fleeting too all hope
And those left alive   lost all
And withdrew to the winding   woeful tunnels
Under the earth   in which
They slowly starved,   no safety they saw
While in the Upground   another danger
Pursued them, made them prey   for a terrible purpose.

The story is hypnotic for Mae as Odile traces the troubles that led up to the Large War and the fire that rained for days over the earth, scorching everything. Then the nonstop wars over food and water, as all the while the earth itself died along with the animals and insects—wars, climate change, and hatred doomed the earth and all who lived on it. How their settlement was all they could rely on to hold back the death that covered the land.

But then in her dream, the song suddenly changes from the history of the tribe to Mae's personal history with Odile. Odile begins to sing about how Odile, though no longer young, captivated Mae. How they became such special friends. How Odile took Mae in, first as a young adept intent on learning how to be a Singer, then as a close and intimate companion.

When Odile ends her song in the traditional way—

Thus truly have I sung   to the tribe this day.

87

—Mae wakes from her dream. At first she is disoriented, the differences between the dream world and her current world being so great . . . It is a world of more death and loss than she could possibly have imagined when she was as young as the girl in her dream. But once she accepts that she is awake, she is confused that the evening light is so strong and bright.

It's the next day, she realizes with a gasp of surprise.

Anya didn't wake her up for her watch!

Mae looks around frantically, then sees Anya sitting cross-legged at the foot of the tree, gazing out at the area around them.

"Have you been up all night?" Mae asks.

Anya gives her peculiar nod.

"Why did you not wake me?"

"Needed sleep."

"But you didn't sleep?" Mae asks.

A casual shrug.

"Anya!"

"Nay worry," Anya says. "But. Look."

She points across the dry rolling fields toward the north. Mae shields her eyes from the sun. "What am I looking for?" she asks.

"There. Settlement?" Anya asks.

Mae looks further into the distance, but sees only the endless brown scrub of dead bushes and trees. "I see nothing," she says.

"There," Anya says, and directs Mae's gaze between two large trees that once were pines, their mottled bark now peeling and dry.

"Entrance to underground," Anya says.

"Yes," Mae says, "that might be the settlement. But how do you know it's there?"

"Passed often, in wandering. Forget, but in daylight remember."

"You passed by the settlement?"

Her cocked nod. "Many times."

"And you never stopped?" Mae asks.

"Nay."

"I wish you had," Mae tells her.

Anya shakes her head. "Nay settler, me."
She slides off of the the tree.
"We go," she says. "Leave now, arrive this night."

21

But they never make it.

They get to within a few klicks of the settlement. They are walking through a dry lake bed when Anya, in the lead, holds a hand out to stop them. She says nothing, but, squinting into the sun, searches the area and sniffs the air.

"What?" Mae asks.

Anya shakes her head and sweeps a hand down low. Silence, her gesture insists.

Anya looks around one more time and draws Mae and Twig in close to her. "Trouble," she whispers. "Follow."

She crouches and leads them up over the river bank and into a stand of dead trees, tall and straight and bunched together. Raggedmen must be nearby, Mae thinks, because Anya continues to swivel her head even though Mae can't see or smell them.

Mae guides Twig by the hand. Twig begins to whine but Mae holds a hand across the girl's mouth and hisses, "Shhh!" Twig goes quiet.

Anya pulls Mae toward her. "Raggedmen," Anya whispers.

"How do you know?" Mae asks.

"I know."

"We're so near the settlement," Mae says. "Can we make it?"

"Nay," Anya says, "raggedmen too near."

Mae sniffs the air but can't smell them—just the dry metallic tinge of the irradiated dirt.

"So what should we do?" Mae asks.

Anya looks around again, thinks for a few moments, then says, "Come," in a low voice Mae can barely make out.

Anya squat-walks to the side of a granite boulder that dips down into an arroyo. Mae stoops and shuffles—she cannot squat the way Anya does—holding onto Twig's hand as she goes.

Anya slides down first and helps Twig down, then Mae.

As quietly as they can, they hunker down behind the boulder. There is a slight rise immediately behind them; the effect is of being in a protected cup. It is not deep, but it will have to do.

"Safe here," Anya says. "Spend night, reach settlement tomorrow. Raggedmen gone by then."

Though she says it with her usual authority, Mae believes it is more hope than certainty.

But Mae says, "Good." She puts an arm around Twig and draws the girl close to her. Twig is trembling though it is very hot. Fear. She may be slow, as her father had said, but she knows danger.

Mae tells her, "All is good. We'll rest here."

Twig squirms, but Mae holds on and finally the girl quiets down.

Anya unwraps the last chunks of meat and hands them to Mae and Twig. She reserves a small half-piece for herself.

"Last food," Anya says.

"We'll get more at the settlement," Mae says, knowing again it is more dim hope than expectation.

She begins to wonder if she should go on by herself, slip through the dim light of the approaching evening to make sure that they will, in fact, accept them there.

She realizes almost immediately that this is a bad idea. Even if she makes it, the guards will likely turn her away—or else kill her outright and she will never get to make her case for accepting Twig and Anya.

No, she must not get separated from her two companions. What the Council in the settlement decides is out of her hands, anyway. It will be better if they all approach the settlement and request entrance together.

That way, the elders will see they have a young girl with them. They will realize at once the importance of that.

Well, maybe.

More hope, again.

She makes herself remember what happened to her the last time she was at her settlement, especially the look of pleasure on Meela's face as her abductor kicked her down after they dragged her out of her sleep chamber and banished her into the Upground. The other security guard, Cyn, was at least apologetic about following the orders of the Council of Elders, but not Meela. Meela seemed to enjoy the hardship she was forcing on Mae. Enjoyed the thought of Mae dragging up in the brutal conditions of the Upground.

But I didn't perish, Mae thinks. I did not just lie there and wait to drag up.

She wonders what the guards at the entrance will say when they see her return. Perhaps Cyn will even be one of them. Then Mae can thank her for leaving the container of water before they abandoned her.

If they don't slay her as soon as they figure out who she is.

She tells Anya she will take the first watch.

As Anya and Twig fall asleep, Mae continues to turn the idea of returning to the settlement over in her mind.

Even if they deny me entrance, she thinks, they will have to admit Anya and Twig. Two new young people will more than make up for Mae, if they should turn her away.

And Mae will have the satisfaction of knowing that she continued to help her tribe survive, regardless of what they did to her.

They will have to be merciful to Twig and Anya.

22

The night passes slowly.

Mae continues to ponder her homecoming.

If they're lucky, Mae decides during the long hours of her watch, there will be Vesters or Vengers out in the morning, looking for treasure or food when the three travelers approach. Neither Vesters nor Vengers are fighters, but as a former Venger she knows that they are always armed with long spears, and all have some defensive training. In the event of trouble with raggedmen, they will be helpful. For all their cruelty, she knows raggedmen are cowards when faced with opposition, especially when they are outnumbered.

That's what was so surprising about the raid on Twig and Ross's settlement. Raggedmen typically don't cooperate like that. It's rare to see more than four together. The large group of raggedmen who were eating together when Mae stumbled on Twig and Ross was even unusual—and probably in preparation for what was to come in the massed attack that destroyed the library.

Mae decides not to disturb Anya when it's time for her to take over the watch. She let me sleep through last night, Mae tells herself, so I will do the same for her. She has been walking all day without any sleep. In case of trouble, Anya is the strongest among the three, and she needs to be as rested and alert as possible.

Unfortunately, Mae also needs to rest, and though she tries to keep herself awake through the quiet night, at some point she falls asleep.

She is awakened by a rough hand scraping across her mouth.

Before she can call out, another hand grabs her cloak at the back of her neck and hauls her up and backwards over the boulder that shields them. She bangs her spine hard on the rockface as she passes over it.

With the hand across her mouth, she cannot scream to warn the others. Her strength is no match for whoever is dragging her from behind. She tries to bite down on the fingers, but cannot get her teeth into anything.

The hand is filthy, bitter-tasting, revolting.

She is dragged away from the boulder and by the time she is dropped on the ground, a hand still holding her sleeve, she sees Twig has also been captured. In the amber sunlight of night she can see a raggedman standing over the girl as the other stands over Mae.

But where is Anya?

A spasm of fear passes through her. Did they kill Anya first, recognizing that she is the biggest danger?

If so, there is no hope for Mae and Twig.

Her thoughts clear and she realizes that she has seen these two before. The one who dragged her off doesn't have a nose, and the other one who is standing over Twig has livid lines of scars framing his face from forehead to chin.

These are the same raggedmen who tried to take Twig several days ago, before Mae rescued her by driving a knife into the belly of the third man.

The two raggedmen are breathing heavily and making deep, guttural noises, almost growls, that stop as they slowly recognize their captives.

A grin spreads across the face of the man with no nose. It is a horrible, feral sight, the ivory bones of his face visible along with the ragged teeth in his mouth.

He pulls up the rags that make up the cloak he is wearing. He has no pants; his legs are boney and as scarred as his face. His pitiful organ hangs down limply, but the primitive gesture of dominance plants even more fear in Mae, as it was meant to.

He looks from Mae down to Twig, on the ground beside him. The girl is paralyzed with fear, her eyes squeezed shut so she can't see the waking nightmare of the man who almost took her once before, who is now preparing to finish the job.

Except the man looks from Twig down to the point of the knife that suddenly protrudes through the front of his coat.

He looks at it in surprise and confusion at first, then his face contracts in pain and he howls.

The point of the knife disappears as quickly as it came. The raggedman clutches the spot where it appeared and drops to his knees. Anya stands behind him with the knife in her hand.

Anya is alive!

She holds the knife over her head in both hands and drives it down into the back of the raggedman on his knees in front of her.

She withdraws the knife and kicks his body sideways.

While her own captor is distracted by watching this, Mae tries to struggle out of his grip. He lets her go and quickly bends to take up his staff from the ground beside him. Before Mae can scuttle away to safety, he swings it down on the back of her head with two quick strikes.

The world explodes in fire inside Mae's head.

Leaving Mae where she fell, the raggedman turns his attention to Anya. He draws his staff back and takes a wild swing at her.

But she is ready for him, and her fighting skills are superior to his. Instead of backing away, Anya drops the knife and jumps forward and catches the staff in both hands and lets the momentum of the raggedman's swing carry him forward and around. She pulls the staff out of his hands and he loses his footing and somersaults to the ground.

Before he can regain his feet, Anya is on him. She drives the sharpened point of the spear into the center of his chest and he is finished.

23

Anya first kneels beside Twig. The girl lies with her hands entwined tightly over her face and her body is stiff and still. Anya rapidly inspects her and, satisfied she is not harmed, turns her attention to Mae.

Mae is not so lucky. She lies on her back with her eyes open staring into the midnight sky. Anya tries to rouse her with soft shakes.

Mae looks up at her but her sight is blurry. Mae thinks Odile is bending over her.

Mae tries to gather herself to rise, but the world careens around her and she finds herself too weak and dizzy to move. Her head is in agony. She has never felt pain like this in her life.

"I'm cold," Mae says. The world is spinning out of control and she has no way to stop it. She wishes Odile would hold her and warm her up.

"I know," Odile says.

Anya parts Mae's clothes but sees no injuries to her.

But Anya saw the raggedman deliver two tremendous blows to Mae's head and heard the crack of bone. Anya gently turns Mae's head and sees the skull glistening through Mae's scalp. Blood oozes from a gaping wound.

There is nothing Anya can do for her.

She lays Mae's head back and sits on her heels. She holds Mae's hands in her own.

"Cold," Mae says again. She begins to shiver.

Anya takes her own cloak off and drapes it over Mae.

"Thank you," Mae tries to whisper, but even to her own ears she can't make sense of the words.

Anya pats Mae's hand.

"Odile," Mae tries to say, and, missing the word, Anya leans closer. Mae's face is grey.

"Take care of Twig," Mae intends to say. Anya can't understand anything except for "Twig." Anya understands Mae is asking her to care for the child.

"Aye," Anya says. "I will."

Mae can only nod slightly. Even that small movement brings white lights exploding behind her eyes.

Emerging out of the brightness, Mae sees Odile's beautiful face, every precious line and wrinkle, coming close to her own. Odile opens her mouth, and Mae hears her companion's final song. As always, Odile's voice is indescribably lovely.

"Listen! Lend me, sister,   leave to sing my song,
Tribe-chest of the tales   that teach our Before.
How this adventure ends   at last is known.
Among the eternal elders   Mae at the end
Assumes the spot   saved for her always
Her conflicts over, calm awaits   in peace she continues.
And thus truly have I sung   to my dearest friend this day.

As Anya watches, Mae closes her eyes and sighs deeply. Then she begins to twitch and jerk violently.

Anya tries to keep her quiet, or at least keep her from hurting herself even more. A final shudder shakes her body. Then she is still.

Anya sits holding Mae's hand, looking for the rise and fall of Mae's chest. But she sees nothing; Mae is gone.

Anya has seen death many times before. She knows she is looking into its face now.

She takes Mae's cloak from around her and lays it over the old woman. It may not keep anyone from disturbing it, but it is all that Anya can do. They need to get moving.

Then she stands and scans the area for any other raggedmen who might be around. She sees none.

She bends over Twig and gently pulls the girl to her feet. She pries Twig's hands away from her face. Anya wraps her arms around the petrified child, cooing softly, and holds her there until she feels the tension leak from Twig's body.

Anya unfolds Twig, and Twig notices Mae's inert body.

Twig points at her and looks to Anya, who shakes her head.

"Mae," Twig commands. "Mae! Up!"

She looks in fury now at Anya.

"Mae nay rise," Anya says.

"No!" Twig cries. She starts for Mae but Anya holds her back and the girl buries her head in the folds of Anya's cloak. Anya lets her howl her agony into the filthy rags.

Then Anya pulls Twig away and says, "Must go. Say bye."

Twig shakes her head, as if refusing to say it will mean Mae is not dead and they won't have to leave her.

But Mae is dead, and they cannot stay. They have to take their leave.

Anya leads Twig by the hand toward Mae. Together they kneel and, following Anya's lead, Twig lays a hand on Mae's head.

"Peace now," Anya says.

"Peace," Twig murmurs, in tears now.

They stay for another few moments, then Anya rises and pulls Twig up. She guides Twig away from where Mae lies. It is not easy; Twig digs her heels into the sand. Anya says, "Must go," and drags Twig until the girl begins to walk on her own.

Anya's first priority is getting them away from the three dead bodies. She leads Twig for a while in the direction they had been going, toward Mae's settlement.

But as they walk, Anya reconsiders.

Showing up at Mae's settlement will not be a good idea, Anya is certain. From her own experiences, Anya doubts they will be welcomed, no matter what Mae's assurances. And even if they are allowed in, fitting in will be impossible for Anya. She has spent most of her life avoiding the restrictions of a settled area—the rules about what to do and how to do it, as well as what not to do, the constant suspicion, the regimentation, the restrictions on how to behave, the filthy menial tasks that outsiders are assigned . . .

She watches Twig tramp along beside her. The only reminder of Twig's distress now a frown on the girl's dirty face.

Anya wonders if that frown will ever leave her.

With her last breath, Mae asked Anya to take care of Twig, and she will. Anya will teach Twig how to survive in what Mae called the Upground as she herself had done since her own family died when she was a girl. Just like Twig. She will teach Twig all she has taught herself about making her way through this world, as she wished someone had been there to teach her.

When the entrance to the settlement comes into sight, Anya turns Twig away from it.

Now Anya is free again to go her own way, as she has always been.

Only this time she will not be alone. She will have Twig with her as student, helper, and companion.

When Twig grows too tired to walk, Anya picks her up and carries her forward into the endless dead, dry land.

Also by Donald Levin

THE MARTIN PREUSS MYSTERY SERIES

CRIMES OF LOVE | BOOK 1

One cold November night, police detective Martin Preuss joins a frantic search for a seven-year-old girl with epilepsy who has disappeared from the streets of his suburban Detroit community. Unwilling to let go after the Oakland County Sheriff's Office takes the case from his city agency, he strikes out on his own, following leads across the entire metropolitan region. Probing deep into the anguished lives of all those who came into contact with the missing girl, Preuss must summon all his skills and resources to solve the many crimes of love he uncovers.

THE BAKER'S MEN | BOOK 2

Easter, 2009. The nation is still reeling from the previous year's financial crisis. Ferndale Police detective Martin Preuss is spending a quiet evening with his son Toby when he's called out to investigate a savage after-hours shooting at a bakery in his suburban Detroit community. Was it a random burglary gone wrong? A cold-blooded execution linked to Detroit's drug trade? Most frightening of all, is there a terrorist connection with the Iraqi War vets who work at the store? Struggling with these questions, frustrated by the dizzying uncertainties of the case and hindered by the treachery of his own colleagues who scheme against him Preuss is drawn into a whirlwind of greed, violence, and revenge that spans generations across metropolitan Detroit.

GUILT IN HIDING | BOOK 3

The third entry in the Martin Preuss mystery series finds Preuss called out to search for a van that has disappeared along with the woman who was driving and her passenger, a handicapped young man. Working through layer upon layer of secrets, Preuss exposes a multitude of contemporary crimes with roots in the twentieth century's darkest period. Complex, chilling, and compulsively readable, *Guilt in Hiding* finds Preuss investigating the most disturbing and unforgettable crimes of his career.

THE FORGOTTEN CHILD | BOOK 4

Newly retired Martin Preuss passes his days quietly with his beloved son Toby. When a friend asks him to look for a boy who disappeared forty years ago, the former investigator gradually becomes consumed with finding the forgotten child. Meanwhile, ex-colleague Janey Cahill persuades him to help her locate the missing father of a troubled young girl. Juggling both cases, Preuss revisits the countercultural fervor of Detroit in the 1970s-and plunges into hidden worlds of guilty secrets and dark crimes that won't stay buried.

AN UNCERTAIN ACCOMPLICE | BOOK 5

Twenty years have passed since Raymond Douglas went to prison for the kidnapping and murder of a local businessman's wife. Now Douglas's daughter has hired private investigator Martin Preuss to track down a previously-unknown accomplice to the crime—who may or may not even exist. But no sooner does Preuss get involved than he finds himself entangled in two murders, a family whose wealth has bought them nothing but trouble, a body discarded in a dumpster, and a web of deceit stretching across metropolitan Detroit from the mega-rich suburbs to a hardscrabble trailer park.

COLD DARK LIES | BOOK 6

When distraught Carrie Morrison hires Martin Preuss to find out how her younger brother wound up clinging to life in a disreputable Ferndale motel, the private detective thinks the story will be a familiar one—a young man takes a walk on the wild side and pays a terrible price. But the deeper Preuss digs, the more he realizes that nothing is as it seems in the brother's world of secrets and lies. How is the young man involved with a missing prostitute? What's the link to a local rap mogul who moonlights as the city's main drug supplier? Why is a stone-cold killer out for revenge with Preuss in his cross-hairs? And—most upsetting of all—why is a local crime boss threatening Preuss's beloved handicapped son Toby?

About the Author

Donald Levin is an award-winning fiction writer and poet. Besides the six books in the Martin Preuss mystery series, he is also a contributor to the anthology of dystopian novellas *Postcards from the Future: A Triptych on Humanity's End*. He is the author of a novel, *The House of Grins*, and two books of poetry, *In Praise of Old Photographs* and *New Year's Tangerine*. He splits his time between Ferndale, Michigan, and West Palm Beach, Florida.